Queen of Hearts

♥

MARTHA BROOKS

Queen of Hearts

Farrar Straus Giroux
New York

First published in Canada by Groundwood Books Limited, 2010
Printed in the United States of America
Designed by Roberta Pressel
First American edition, 2011
1   3   5   7   9   10   8   6   4   2

macteenbooks.com

Library of Congress Cataloging-in-Publication Data
Brooks, Martha, 1944–
    Queen of hearts / Martha Brooks. — 1st American ed.
        p.   cm.
    Summary: Shortly after her first kiss but before her sixteenth birthday in
December, 1941, Marie Claire and her younger brother and sister are sent
to a tuberculosis sanatorium near their Manitoba farm.
    ISBN: 978-0-374-34229-6
    [1. Tuberculosis—Fiction.   2. Sick—Fiction.   3. Hospitals—Fiction.
4. Coming of age—Fiction.   5. Family life—Manitoba—Fiction.
6. Manitoba—History—20th century—Fiction.   7. Canada—History—
1914–1945—Fiction.]   I. Title.

PZ7.B7975Que 2011
[Fic]—dc22

                                                                    2010052661

I am certain of nothing but the holiness of the heart's affections and the truth of imagination.

—*John Keats*

For my imaginative editors,
Melanie Kroupa and Shelley Tanaka,
in friendship, kinship, and sisterhood

Author's Note

I grew up in a medical family on the grounds of a tuberculosis sanatorium in Ninette, Manitoba, where my father was a thoracic surgeon and my mother a nurse. As a kid, I'd tear down the hilly road on my bike, black Lab yapping at the wheels. Patients, both young and old, pressed their faces against the balcony screens and laughed and called down to me to stop to talk. I'd come to an abrupt halt, back up the bike, crane my neck, and then we'd chat. I was lonely. They missed their families. It was perfect.

At the beginning of the last century, tuberculosis caused over one-third of the deaths in young people ages fifteen to thirty-five. Imagine being sixteen years old, contracting TB, and then being confined to a long-term care facility. How would one respond? It was a question I wanted answered, fictionally.

Queen of Hearts takes place a few years before I was born, also at a time just before the arrival of the "miracle drugs," as the first antibiotics were known—streptomycin being the earliest. As a treatment for TB, these drugs seemed to promise a permanent end to the disease and helped many beat back their illness. Up until then, rest and good food were the mainstays of "chasing the cure," as well as various types of "collapse therapy." These were simply the best tools and techniques medical people worked with.

During the three years and many drafts that it took to find my characters and try to catch them in all those revelatory human moments that are the mark of good fiction, I struggled with my own health issues. At one point, I found myself lying in a hospital bed with a traumatically induced collapsed lung. I had almost died, but the wonderful thing was the collapsed lung. I had just written about it in *Queen of Hearts* and I'd wondered how it felt. Well, what fabulous research! When you read Marie-Claire's own experience with collapse therapy, think of me!

As World War II was being waged overseas, the crusade back home to lick TB presented a fierce challenge. This book is a valentine to the foot soldiers of that righteous war—doctors, nurses, other staff, and especially the amazing patients who sought victory over their disease and sometimes won and sometimes didn't.

Sixty years on, the fight against TB is anything but over. In fact, experts say there is now more tuberculosis than ever before in human history, and new drug-resistant strains of the bacterium have appeared around the world, including in North America. The disease kills about two million people annually, mainly in impoverished third world countries.

Wolf at the Door

Summer 1940

ONE

On a cold evening in late spring, with the rain coming down hard around him, there's Oncle Gérard standing outside our farmhouse just like he's never been away.

Twenty-five years old and a pile of bones, Papa's younger brother has been riding the rails since he was nineteen. Last we heard, with a war starting in Europe and Canada getting involved, he tried to enlist in the army. They wouldn't take him, so we thought he was still hopping boxcars to heaven knows where, living the hobo life.

But here's Maman opening the door to him as he pulls a dripping, battered hat from his head. Dark damp curls fall onto his forehead just like on that little movie clown, Charlie Chaplin.

"Hello, Sylvie," are the first words out of his mouth. Then, with a magnificent sweep, he hands our mother some red tulips he's been hiding behind his back—flowers I recognize from our own garden.

I laugh. Maman, too.

"Always so thoughtful," she says, ushering him in out of the rain.

She plunges the flowers into a pitcher of water before setting them in the middle of the table.

"Come and sit. Eat with us, Gérard. There's plenty. Henri and the hired man are down at the barn, and Luc's there with them. They'll be coming up soon. Luc's grown—he was ten last February—you won't recognize him. Marie-Claire, set another place for your uncle."

Oncle Gérard winks playfully at me. He's unshaven and missing a few more teeth since the last time I saw him—two years ago, when I was twelve—but I'd know him anywhere.

"You've grown, too, Marie-Claire. Last time I saw you, you were—this high."

He gently teases his hand lower, lower, and lower still, until it's only inches from the floor.

I laugh at this, too. It's fun to see him again.

He turns and smiles at little Josée getting up on her own chair beside him. She looks into his face. "How big was I?"

He chuckles and shows her his thumb and forefinger, making the smallest gap between them.

"Really? Did I fit in your pocket?"

"Oh yes, yes, of course," he says, happily.

"She's six," I explain.

Just then Papa and Luc and our elderly hired man,

Ambroise LaGare, appear, kicking off their rubber boots at the door.

Oncle Gérard lifts his eyes from Josée. His smile freezes on his face.

"Hello, Henri. Long time no see."

"What are you doing here?" Papa frowns, puts his hand on Luc's shoulder.

"I'd like to visit for a while, if I might. Things, lately, have not been so good for me."

Luc looks over at Oncle Gérard, then up at Papa. "Who's he?"

"Don't be rude, Luc," says Maman. "Don't you remember Papa's brother, your uncle Gérard?"

"The hobo?"

Oncle Gérard throws back his head and laughs.

"Ah me," he says at last. "I like this one already. He's honest."

After supper, our uncle's hands shake as he carefully rolls three cigarettes. He seems to shrug his shoulders a great amount, as if apologizing. He also has a bad cough, which sends tobacco flying everywhere. Finally he gives a cigarette each to Papa and Ambroise, hangs the other from the side of his own mouth, strikes a match with his thumb and forefinger, and lights all three cigarettes. Then, like a tired yet still jaunty old man, he shakes out the flame.

He stays with us one week, then two, then more as the weeks stretch through the summer. Sometimes we sit together on the hill after supper—all us kids with Gérard, the biggest kid of all.

He shows us how to make bird sounds with our hands while we wait for an imaginary monster to come through the gully below our farm.

"The Shadow Man!" Oncle Gérard finally announces like a circus ringmaster. He rises up on his skinny legs. "See the giant with arms as big as tree branches! See his head of hair that holds a hundred birds! See his long loooong shadow . . ."

"But doesn't he eat children? He does, doesn't he?" Josée yanks at his pant leg.

"Ah Josée"—our uncle nods wisely—"of course he eats children. Especially little girls who won't close their eyes at night."

He sits down again.

Josée closes her eyes tight.

"I sleep," she says. "I'm sleeping now."

Luc puts an arm around her shoulders and whispers, "You can *still* see him!"

Josée's brown eyes fly wide open as Luc and I fall over laughing.

Josée scrambles up against Oncle Gérard, who gathers her into his arms and says, "The Shadow Man, he's half human and half ghost, Josée. He can be anywhere, anytime. He can even change shape when he wants to fly."

All at once a hawk circles far above us in the golden light of late day and makes its eerie cry.

"Ohhh!" says Josée. "How does he do that?"

"It's magic," says Luc with a sly look at me.

"That's right." Oncle Gérard musses up Luc's hair and gets to his feet.

"Where are you going?" I ask.

"To town."

"And what are you going to do when you get there?"

"None of your beeswax." He grins.

"Ha, ha," I say. "I'm going to follow you."

"Are you now, my little queen of hearts. I wouldn't advise it, not today."

"It's boring without you, you know," I say, snapping my once-white ankle socks so that gray dust flies everywhere in a satisfying manner.

Oncle Gérard stands smiling down at me, not answering, weaving a little as if his body still remembers the whiskey he consumed last week, when he staggered home at five in the morning and passed out on the bed he shares with Luc.

"You're hopping the train to St. Felix?" I ask.

He nods and casts his restless eyes to the distance.

Twice a day an actual monster, a big long steam train, comes chugging through the gully, slowing down at the steep curve. If you happen to be right there, you can pull yourself up onto one of those boxcars and get a free ride to town. Luc and I are not supposed to do this, but of course we do anyway.

Today neither of us follows Oncle Gérard. He has

serious drinking on his mind. He isn't planning to come back within a few hours, smiling and smelling of alcohol. He's probably going to disappear into next week and then return to us reeking of it.

Papa, as usual, will yell at him and threaten to kick him out. But it won't happen, because, as Maman says, "That Gérard, he's a charmer."

TWO

Our farm is a few miles northwest of the village of St. Felix, Manitoba. On the other side of the valley—a short haul by car or several minutes longer if you hop the train—is the Pembina Hills Tuberculosis Sanatorium. The buildings, built into the hills that hug Pembina Lake, glow at night with all their electric lights. It's then that the whole place looks like a great ship on the prairies. This would be a cheerful sight if it weren't for the fact that so many people, sick with TB, have gone to the San to die.

TB sneaks up to your back door and howls like a hungry wolf that nobody saw coming. That's why people in the community are scared of it. Papa's sister, Tante Angeline, is so scared, in fact, that she drives past the San and instructs her children to cover their noses! I swear to God, this is true.

I'm in the back seat, keeping an eye on my little cousin Laurent. We're at the side of the valley, where the road starts winding down past Pembina Hills San.

Laurent pulls his shirt up over his nose and tells me to do the same.

I say, "Don't be stupid," reach over, and roll down the window.

Quick as anything, Tante Angeline turns in the driver's seat and snaps, "Marie-Claire, you crazy girl, you roll up that window now!"

I want to stick my head out and wave my arms around just to annoy her. Except she jams on the brakes. She's not going any farther, not until I've rolled it back up.

After that my cousin shifts in the seat beside me.

"You're gonna get it." His taunt is muffled by his shirt. "You're gonna get TB, ha, ha."

But by fall, to our terrible surprise, the wolf has slipped past our door and gone straight to Oncle Gérard.

Yet even after his TB is diagnosed, he stays on with us, because where else can he go? Pembina Hills San puts him on a waiting list, saying that there are no available beds and they are already overcrowded.

So Luc, who has always been prone to chest complaints, is banished from his old room as Maman fusses and clucks around. In a sulk he bunks in with Josée and me.

My brother and sister are no longer allowed to see Oncle Gérard. Once in a while, though, when Maman is too exhausted to continue, I'm sent upstairs with a tray of food for him, always with the caution that I'm not to take any more time than necessary. He's been getting sicker—even having to be helped by Maman with his bathroom activities, which embarrasses them both—yet, especially lately, it's always a fresh shock to see him. He looks like a skeleton resting against the pillows.

The morning that word comes of an empty bed at the San, a windy October day that rattles the windows, I'm sent up with a breakfast of toast, fried egg, and a cup of Maman's bitter dark coffee.

The bedroom door is slightly ajar. I use my hip to bump it wider. I enter the room, and he manages to sit up as I go to him and set the tray on the bed across his knees.

His breathing is an effort. Yet he manages to ask playfully, "Will you sit, my queen of hearts?"

"With pleasure."

At this, he relaxes.

Truth be told, I sneak in a visit whenever I can. He's family, after all, and I'm going to miss him. He's always been something of a daredevil, like me. Although it must be said that TB has knocked the daredevil right out of him.

I pull up the single wooden chair that has been left in the otherwise bare room. Everything else has been taken out and furiously cleaned by Maman.

I sit near him and smile into his face. "Eat your toast, at least, *mon oncle*."

"Aren't you afraid to be here with me?" he whispers, serious now. "Aren't you scared of TB?"

"I'm not going to get it," I say, not once taking my eyes from his. "Besides, it only hits old men like yourself!"

His sunken eyes crinkle at the corners and he picks up the toast. He bites into one corner, quickly sets it down again, and bows his head.

I think, at first, that he's praying. Then I realize his shoulders are shaking. He's crying.

"I'm sorry," he says between broken sobs.

"Don't be!"

I pull a clean handkerchief from my pocket and give it to him.

He takes it, slowly wipes his eyes, and lets his hands fall onto his bony knees, which stick up like stumps under the covers.

The wind continues to lash against Maman's gleaming windows.

He says at last, "I'm done for . . . and . . . I'm scared."

So frank and so bleak, just like that.

I excuse myself and go into my bedroom. I pull a cigar box out from the bottom of the dresser drawer. Inside I keep a beautiful hawk feather and a small roll of red satin ribbon in perfect condition that I'm saving for a special occasion. And, because of its mystery, the thing I love most of all: a silver chain with a St. Christopher's medal and a heart dangling alongside it that I found when I was walking in the field one day, brought home and put away, and told nobody about. I take it out every so often and polish it in secret so that it glows, all the while wondering who it once belonged to, how the person lost it, making up stories about it to amuse myself.

I take this chain to Oncle Gérard. I place it, warm from my hand, into his.

"What's this?" he asks, startled.

"It's to give you courage. But you have to say that you'll wear it. Promise me, Oncle."

He nods, looking first at me with red eyes, then at what he now holds in his hand.

Two hours later he leaves us, leaning his shoulder against the passenger window of the car, his battered gray hat slapped in place. He turns his head and fingers the chain with the heart at his chest. His eyes hold me in a long, hard last look as the car slowly pulls out of the yard.

Later, when Papa returns, we hang around him in the kitchen, waiting for him to say something. But he just looks up at us from his place at the end of the kitchen table.

"He's gone. That's it. There's nothing more to say about it."

After that, he goes out to the yard. We hear him into the night, long after we've all gone to bed, furiously chopping logs, adding to a pile of wood that's halfway up the side of the house by morning.

Tante Angeline drops by for a visit. She sits with Maman at the kitchen table, her back to the woodstove—the warmest place in the whole house. She shivers as Maman pours strong hot tea into a rose-patterned cup with a chipped handle.

"Poor Gérard," Tante Angeline says, turning away from her tea to blow her nose. "I suppose they'll make him sleep outside at night with all the others on those balconies. Even in thirty below zero weather."

"He has his own room," Maman tells her. "They don't put him onto the balcony. He's too sick to take the air."

"Oh well," Tante Angeline continues. "And I suppose he drinks a lot of milk now. Aren't they supposed to drink it for their cure? Does he drink milk, Sylvie?"

"Angeline," says Maman with a fierce look, "your brother is, quite possibly, dying. There's not much hope for him in milk."

Like Papa, Tante Angeline never visits Oncle Gérard. Only Maman does, and Papa never wants her to go. Gas is precious these days, what with the war rationing, and why waste her time on trips to visit Gérard anyway, he reasons—unreasonably.

"He made his bed, now let him lie in it."

"Henri," Maman replies, "you don't have to go. Nobody's asking you to go. Only I am going."

At this, she pulls off her apron and throws it at him. He catches it about mid-chest. She stretches out her hand and, as always, he sheepishly gives over the keys. She lifts her coat from the hook by the door and leaves.

"Well?" I say, each time she returns.

"He's a little better, today," she says. Or, "He's a little worse." Never offering more information.

One time I ask, "Why can't I go with you when you visit? Why can't I go and see him for myself?"

"They have rules, Marie-Claire. No children can come to the wards."

"I'm not a child! I'll be fifteen in three weeks. Isn't fifteen old enough?"

She gives me a look. "I only want to keep you safe. And in answer to your question, no."

So on a Saturday morning in early December, I put on her old fur coat, which she wears only on Sundays. I think it will make me look older. I sneak out of the house, run across the yard, then wade through the deep snow in the gully. I reach the railway tracks just as I hear the train coming.

I also hear Luc shouting after me. "Marie-Claire! Wait! Where are you going?"

I turn to him. He's come away from the house wearing only a shivery thin jacket, but he's managed, somehow, to lace up his moccasins.

The train squeals along the tracks and slows, making its way down through the gully. For the next three minutes or so, we'll be able to walk faster than it can roll.

"I'm going to see Oncle Gérard," I tell Luc over the noise of the train as he catches up.

"I'm coming with you."

"Suit yourself." I shrug. "But they're not going to let you on the wards."

"I don't care. I'm coming."

There's a step on the corner of each boxcar and above that an iron grab bar. You stand still and wait for the train to start sliding by, then you grab hold of the bar, letting the momentum of the train swing you onto the step.

A man passing through last summer wasn't so lucky. He lost his balance and the train dragged him under.

Luc and I have made it onto the train dozens of times. Today I confidently swing on first. Around the corner of the step is a ladder. I climb to the top of the boxcar, with my brother right behind me.

Once safely on top, we sink down together. But as the train slowly picks up speed, an icy wind begins to whip by, and I realize we've never done this before in the winter.

It's bitterly cold and I open up Maman's fur coat for Luc to get inside with me. He shakes his head. Acting like a tough boy.

The train chugs along through the snow, up and down hills, past frozen fields, our breath steaming up around us, smoke from the black steam engine curling by. Skinny Luc has at least worn a scarf, but soon it's crusted with ice, and he shivers violently in his stupidly thin jacket.

When we arrive at St. Felix, there's a twenty-minute stop. We lie down flat so we won't be seen, as all the boxcars shunt and squeal and rock, and the workers at the little station house below cry out to one another, unloading freight, loading up more.

We finally get going again. The ride from St. Felix to the Pembina Hills San is going to be another twenty minutes. By now Luc's whimpering with the cold.

"Get over here now!" I order between chattering teeth.

He finally joins me inside Maman's fur coat, a coat that has been passed down to her from our magnificently fat grand-mère. Still, the cold grips us. By the time the train pulls up to the crossing at Pembina Hills San, I can no longer feel my fingers, my toes, or my face.

We scramble off at the little station. As soon as our feet hit the ground I begin to walk up the road as fast as I can go, with Luc marching right along beside me.

The main building blasts heat onto our faces the minute we open the doors. I get us both safely inside, almost fainting from relief.

"Sit over there," I say to my brother.

He sinks, shivering, into a big brown couch in the foyer, and I go to find somebody to talk to about seeing Oncle Gérard.

I find an enclosed office with a windowlike opening that faces the hallway. A man leans lazily against the counter ledge there, waiting for something. He turns and gives me the once-over. I pull the fur coat more firmly around me, as I've so often seen Maman do, and march straight up to the window. I lean in to the switchboard operator at her desk inside the office and announce, "My name is Angeline Bruneau and I'm here to see my brother, Gérard Côté."

She gives me a cool look, takes off her headphones, and pulls three snakelike connectors from the switchboard before she mutters, "Not today."

"I beg your pardon?"

"Sunday is visiting day."

"That's tomorrow!"

"Come back then," she says, turning back to the switchboard.

I can see that I'll have to throw myself at her mercy.

"I came all this way by train—from Montreal!" I cry. "That's thousands of miles! I can't leave now. Besides, my brother is dying and"—I lower my voice—"he's not expected to live out the day."

This last part seems to get her attention. Her shoulders soften slightly.

"Who did you say your brother is?"

I repeat his name. She turns away, consults a list of names in a fat folder, then picks up her pencil and writes something down. At last she gets up out of her chair, walks over, and hands me a slip of yellow paper.

"Second floor of the east infirmary," she says. "His is the first room to your right, as you come up the stairs. Make sure you take this permission slip to the front desk and check in with the head nurse before—"

"Thanks!" I say, already rushing back to Luc.

He's sitting in the same place where I left him. He looks up at me with big miserable eyes. "Leave me Maman's coat, Marie-Claire. I'm still dying of cold."

"You're not dying. You're the one who wanted to come. And I need the coat."

"Did you bring anything to eat at least? I'm starving."

He can be such a pain sometimes. I pull the paper-wrapped sandwich that I'd been planning to eat later out of my pocket. I think about tearing off half for me, but suddenly I've lost my appetite.

Handing him the whole thing, I say, "Well, I'm going now."

"Then go. Who's stopping you?" He shoves the sandwich into his mouth.

Truth is, I've come this far, gotten away with it, but now I don't know what to expect.

I turn and walk outside anyway, squaring my shoulders against the bone-numbing wind, making my way down the narrow icy sidewalk. Soon I reach the east infirmary, open the doors, and step inside. The entire place smells of antiseptic and cleaning fluids and sickness.

I hear coughing at the top of the stairs. I make myself disappear inside the fur coat, covering my face with the big collar. The stairs creak loudly as I cling to the wall and climb to the second floor. Halfway down the long hallway, I see a nurse leave the front desk. She turns and floats away into one of the rooms farther down the hall. I sneak through the door of the first room on my right.

The room is tiny, with a window that looks onto the wintry tops of trees. He seems to be sleeping. He's even thinner than before. Can anyone be so thin and still be alive?

There's no chair for visitors, so I sit on the edge of the bed and take his limp hand.

"Oncle," I say, "it's me, Marie-Claire."

His skin is flushed with fever, his eyelids a waxy yellow. They flutter open. At the sight of me, tears well up and roll down the sides of his face.

Barely above a whisper, he says, "So you made it, my little queen of hearts. I knew you would."

I'm crying now, too. "You don't have to talk," I tell him. "I'll just stay here for a while with you."

He gives a slight nod, and all at once I'm so very glad I came.

After that there's nothing remarkable about our visit, or the place. Just me sitting there holding his hand. I notice he isn't wearing the chain with the medal and the heart I gave him, but maybe that doesn't matter anymore.

Before I leave, I lean in and kiss his cheek and say goodbye. I don't make any promises about trying to come back again. In my heart I know this is the last time.

I pull the fur coat around me once more, slip out of his room like a shadow, and leave the building. Nobody has seen me come or go. The winter air's as sharp as ever, but I'm glad to smell it, and even more glad to be walking around in it.

When I get back to the main building, there's Maman, sitting with her arm resting along the back of the sofa behind Luc. He rolls his eyes at me.

Maman stands up and makes Luc do the same. She is furious.

"Let's go," she says, looking me up and down in Grand-mère's fur.

"I drove over here knowing that I might find you. What were you thinking, Marie-Claire? Hopping the train in the middle of winter. You could have slipped on the ice and killed yourselves under the wheels. Not to mention the cold. Just look at the way your brother is dressed!"

With that she marches us out the door.

The following week, Luc and I both catch the flu. A couple of weeks later, mine turns to bronchitis, his to some kind of croup that goes on and on. But that doesn't seem unusual, because he's always coming down with one thing or another.

As for Oncle Gérard, he takes a long while to die, finally passing away in early February, just after Luc's eleventh birthday.

THREE

When I was born, I'm told that Papa looked at Maman and said, "Oh well, the next one will be a boy." Two miscarriages later, Maman finally gave birth, early, to tiny Luc, and Papa got his wish.

Me, I've always been as healthy as a horse. Even after getting the flu that turned to bronchitis after the train incident, you wouldn't think from looking at me that there's anything wrong.

Luc, on the other hand—always a thin pale kid that Papa and Maman coddle—is in bed for weeks. He only emerges from his cave of a room on Pancake Tuesday, the day before Ash Wednesday.

"What are you giving up for Lent?" Josée asks as he joins us at the supper table.

"Nothing," says Luc, reaching to dig his fork into a pile of pancakes on a platter. He helps himself to five. "If I go to hell, I won't go hungry."

"Watch your tongue," says Maman.

"Glad to see you've got back your hollow leg there, son," Papa says with a smile, passing him the syrup.

Easter comes and goes. Spring turns to summer and school is over. Then, just as summer work on the farm begins, Ambroise tells Papa, "I'm too old for this work."

Within the week, he's packed up what little he owns and gone to live in town with his spinster sister.

All the able young hired men are enlisted in the war by now. There's no help to be found. And Luc, he's always off shooting gophers for five cents a tail, saving up for that bicycle our parents couldn't afford to get him at Christmas.

"The boy still has a cough; leave him be," Papa says to Maman. "Marie-Claire's a good strong girl. She doesn't mind helping out."

It's nice to be told I'm a good strong girl, and it's true, I don't mind. I've always helped out, except now I'll do more.

I'm up at five every morning, milking the cows with Papa, laying my sleepy head against their soft flanks as the hot milk sings into the pail.

We carry the milk into the house, where Maman works the cream separator. Papa and I go back out to the barn, feed the animals, shovel out manure, and put down fresh straw. I set Josée to the task of gathering eggs while sometimes I kill any chickens the family can spare and get them ready for market or our own table.

Maman bakes all our bread and buns and pies in the

blasting heat of the wood-burning stove. I'm there helping her when I'm not with Papa out in the fields.

And then, of course, I can read for long hours by my window, where the sun on the long northern nights hardly ever seems to go to bed, either.

As luck would have it, there's an army base near St. Felix. The soldiers come to town in their smart uniforms and shiny boots and flirt with all the girls.

One Saturday, my friend Yvette LaBossière tells somebody named Floyd—Floyd from Parry Sound, Ontario—that we're both eighteen.

"Is that a fact?" He grins. "I had you girls pegged for jailbait for sure."

He's come up to us as we're standing outside Drapeau's grocery and meat shop. Papa's brought a turkey and a goose to town and has just taken them around the back of the building to Drapeau's stainless-steel smoker.

Yvette looks into Floyd's eyes—eyes that gobble her up from head to toe. "You going to the dance at the hall tonight?" she asks.

"Sure thing." He turns to me, all smiles. "I got a buddy named Joe. He'd like you."

"Oh really?" I glance down at my feet, then back at Floyd. "How do I know that I'd like him?"

Floyd looks over at Yvette, then back at me. "So my buddy needs a date, too. Maybe we'll see you girls later."

He walks away in his big black boots.

24

Yvette says, "You know what your problem is? You're too picky."

She's the kind of girl who is always more than happy to point out your problems to you. At least she's honest, which is why she's my friend. I wait for more, and then it comes. "And you're too old-fashioned. You'd look better if you wore some lipstick. Ditch those dowdy clothes."

Yvette makes her own clothing out of practically nothing. Another thing I like about her. Show her the smallest slash of pretty cloth and it'll find its way into a skirt border or a blouse collar or a scarf. That Yvette, she's clever.

Just then, along comes her oldest brother, Marc.

He gives us a wide smile and lowers to the sidewalk his giggling four-year-old daughter, whom he's been carrying around under his big golden arm. She flings her own arms around her young papa's legs and looks up at him as he puts his hand on her head and proudly tells Yvette and me, "I've just enlisted in the army."

When I was four and Marc was twelve, he taught me how to skate at the outdoor rink in town. He backed me securely against his long legs. Then he moved us out across the ice. We glided together at first, getting the feel of it, but before long I was standing alone weaving around like an awkward duck.

"Marc, look at me!" I said just before I fell on my butt.

He laughed as he skated up again, pulling me to my feet and setting me off by myself once more.

When winter comes, who will teach his own little girl to skate?

"Let's go, squirt," he says, picking her up again. "Bye, you two."

We watch them disappear into Drapeau's.

Yvette, at first rubbing her eyes as if they are sore, finally turns to me and says, "I'm going to that dance tonight. I'm going to dance like there's no tomorrow. And I don't care if you come or not."

Later, Maman tells me, "Well, you're not going. There'll be plenty of time for dances and boyfriends, Marie-Claire."

"How can you say that? Papa was your boyfriend when you were both fifteen."

"That was a different time," replies Maman, flattening her lips.

I can't argue with her. Lately there's desperation in the air. We all know girls who, as the crude saying goes, hit the mattress every night with some soldier. The war has begun to change everything as we watch the local boys leave, draining our community of available romance. And then the Saturday night dances, the St. Felix girls, and all those soldiers from away. Sometimes there are engagements, quick marriages.

"That Yvette, she's playing with fire," Maman warns me. "Before you know it, she'll be in a family way. Nice girls don't go out with soldiers, Marie-Claire."

I figure I'm a nice girl but decide to sneak out that

night anyway. I'll walk to town and join up with Yvette and Floyd and Joe-whoever-he-is at the dance hall. First I put on my one good dress, a cream-colored faille that hugs every curve of my body. Next I dig out the cigar box and take out the red satin ribbon I've been saving. I tie back my curly brown hair with it, lean into the mirror, pinch my cheeks for color, and catch Josée's reflection behind me.

I turn. She's standing in her pink nightgown, brushing her own glossy hair in imitation of me.

She looks so much like me that she takes my breath away. Papa may have gotten his boy, but Maman got two girls cut from the same cloth.

"Where are you going, Marie-Claire? Are you going to a movie? Can I come?"

Our grocery store proprietor, Mr. Drapeau, is also the projectionist at the town hall, where they show movies every Friday night.

I pull Josée to sit on the bed beside me.

"It's Saturday, remember?"

"Oh," she says.

"I'm going to a dance," I say, hugging her.

"A dance? Will there be music?"

I laugh. "Of course. There's always music at dances."

She looks at me with her big eyes. "Can I come with you? I love music!"

"Not tonight. And this will be our little secret, okay? Don't tell Maman."

"What if she comes and asks where you are?"

"I'll be back," I say with a wink, "before it's time to milk the cows in the morning. Nobody will be any the wiser. The cows won't tell, if you won't."

Soon I shimmy out our bedroom window and down the ladder I placed earlier against the north wall. I jump to the ground, turn the ladder on its side, stash it in the tall prairie grasses, and run for the road.

Dust swirls up around my ankles. It's a hot night. Nine o'clock, and the setting sun still sits over the hills. From the bottom of our lane, where it joins up with the winding gravel road, I can see the little town of St. Felix in the distance and, far across the lake, Pembina Hills San, with its shiplike lights that are now beginning to blink on in the evening air.

Thirty-three minutes later, I'm in town. The doors to the hall have been thrown open. Several soldiers and their dates linger, laughing, outside. White moths flutter against the lamp over the door. A car pulls out of the parking lot, its windows steamed up—a telltale sign that the couple inside have been necking and fooling around.

I walk into the hall, and a saxophone wails across the dance floor over the heads of all the dancers. The cigarette smoke is so thick that it, too, fogs up the air.

"Marie-Claire!"

I turn, and there's Yvette in a yellow dress so bright it hurts the eyes. She's tucked under Floyd's arm, happy to see me, very drunk. Floyd's drunk, too, though not quite so much.

A shy boy, army cap tipped over his forehead, is standing behind them. He isn't drunk. I figure this is Joe.

For the next few hours I dance with him. He smells like wool and Old Spice aftershave, and his whiskers, which are dark, graze my cheek when he pulls back his head to look at me.

"Boy, you're beautiful," he says, looking into my eyes, and I suddenly feel that I am.

He's a perfect gentleman, holding me lightly in his arms, while his hands, which are slippery with sweat like mine, tremble with emotion.

Just before all the soldiers have to leave to go back to the base, Joe buys me a bottle of pop and we go outside to sit on the hall steps. We sit close. I don't know a thing about him, but his shyness is nice. He tells me they'll be shipping out before long and then, cigarette smoke wreathing his head, he asks, "Will you write to me, Marie-Claire?"

"Sure," I answer, reaching down to scratch my ankle where a mosquito has bitten it.

"That would be swell," he says with a sigh, as if the thought of getting letters from me, a girl he doesn't know, makes going to war easier somehow. And then he says, "Can I kiss you?"

What is the sense in refusing a little kiss? There won't be much kissing where he's going.

"Sure," I say again, sitting up and turning to him.

He gathers me into his arms and his lips are soft and

it's a very nice kiss. Not the kind I dream of late at night in my bedroom with my pillow, imagining I'm kissing a movie star, but nice enough for a first kiss.

"I'll remember that kiss" is the last thing he says to me.

I walk home under the stars, proud in my heart that I'm the girl who has given Joe something to think about over-seas, besides lifting his gun to kill somebody.

My body is suddenly tired, too tired to move quickly. Anyway, there's no need to rush.

I finally get back to the farm in the wee hours of the morning. I crawl back through the window, fall down in bed, sweating in the airless room I share with Josée, and then listen to her soft breathing and wait for the birds to start chirping.

Soon enough they do—a thousand or so, it seems—and then a lone cow starts to bellow. It's time to get up again.

FOUR

Sister Thérèse, walking by my desk with her yardstick, pokes me awake on several occasions throughout the fall and early winter. One December day she keeps me after school. She stretches her long legs in front of her, her cracked black shoes showing below her long black skirts. Sister Thérèse and I love and hate each other in equal measures.

Today I love her. I wasn't looking forward to walking home through the snow and then going directly to the barn, so I'm happy for this delay. My hands, like her shoes, are cracked—and red. My nose drips.

Because we're alone she can let down her guard. She has an orange in her pocket, which she pulls out and slowly peels. She offers me half. I haven't seen an orange since last Christmas. Every winter the nuns are sent a crate of them from somewhere.

I quietly eat my half of the orange while she eats hers.

"You used to be a gifted student, Marie-Claire," she

says at last. She uses words like that when we are alone, too.

I shrug.

"What's wrong with you this year? Why are you always sleeping in class?"

"I don't know."

"You don't sleep at night?"

The smell of orange fills the dusty schoolroom.

"Perhaps you are missing Yvette," she says, with the tiniest sniff of disapproval.

Yvette LaBossière, who got pregnant just as Maman predicted, was sent to live with her aunt in Winnipeg in the early fall. One day she was here, the next she was gone. She could at least have said goodbye to me, but she didn't. So much for our friendship.

I shrug again. I have another cold, and these days I never feel well. This, more than anything, makes me sorry for myself. What can I tell her? It would only sound like complaining, and I'm too proud to complain.

She heaves a big sigh, shakes her head, gets to her feet, and says, "Whatever it is, say your prayers, Marie-Claire. God is always listening."

Papa, of course, is already at the barn when I get home. He turns to me.

"Where have you been? You were supposed to be here an hour ago."

I pretend I haven't heard him and set up my milking

stool. I think about the V-mail that I got yesterday from Joe. He's written three letters to my three, so now we're even. He's stationed somewhere in England. He says he's made friends with a local farm family.

Dairy and the family could use a couple of extra hands so I'm usually there helping out on my days off. Other than that we're all bored here waiting for something to happen. Guess I should have joined the navy or the air force. As for all us regular army stiffs it's nothing but drills and training and more training for stuff we already know. Our pup tents leak and English winters are cold and the sun's forgot about us. Oh yeah and the food they give us isn't fit for a goat. Well, enough of my griping— but I'm mailing this letter off the base anyway so they won't censor it. By the way thanks for your last letter. Every night when I close my eyes I know I'll see your face in my dreams. It keeps me going.

Yours truly,
Joe

"Didn't you hear me?" Papa's standing over me. His rubber boots and his pant legs are covered in muck and bits of straw. "What's wrong with you these days?"

"Nothing," I mumble, and start with Jessie. She's a big one, and as she relaxes, letting her milk down—the rhythm of it drumming into the pail—I think about her life, which isn't so bad. As for my own, it isn't so bad, either, when you really look at it. It's just that it seems it should somehow be happier than all this day in, day out drudgery. And now I'm jealous of an English farm family I don't even know because they have Joe to help them out once in a while.

Later, sitting at the kitchen table, I pick away at my supper. Sister Thérèse has started me wondering why these days my body feels like lead all the time, but then Josée has also been droopy with a series of bugs. Tonight she feeds carrots under the table to our fat dog, Didier, who isn't even supposed to be inside the house, being a good farm dog.

Maman doesn't seem to notice. Her worried eyes catch Papa's every so often. She jumps in her chair when Luc, upstairs in bed, starts another round of coughing.

"He's always sick," Papa says, lowering his mouth to his fork.

"He's caught another chill," Maman explains. "And now the doctor says he has the croup again. But he had the croup last month. How can he have it again?"

"He hasn't been right all year," says Papa. "Not since that first chill." He tosses a quick look at me.

Of course he's thinking about Luc and me hopping the train together. Is it my fault that his precious son does as he pleases? Why am I to blame for his bad health?

"I don't know why this keeps happening," continues Maman. "I don't know what to think. Who do you believe if you can't believe your own doctor?"

"Dr. McTavish is senile, Maman," I interrupt. "He's the worst doctor in the world. Why do you even listen to him?"

"Maybe Luc has TB," says little Josée, kicking her legs against her chair, sending Didier on scattering paws to the porch door off the kitchen.

She bends innocently over her plate as silence fills the house. Even Luc has stopped coughing.

Papa suddenly drops his fork, tears off a heel of bread, and says, "No son of mine will be touched by that plague."

Three days later, Luc coughs up bright foamy blood all over himself, his bedclothes, and our frightened mother's apron.

As if Papa could have stopped it! But none of us is prepared for the shock of what happens next.

Two Terrible Weeks
in December

Christmas 1941

FIVE

Luc is hit the worst. Yet, soon enough, chest X-rays also show TB shadows invading the lungs of Josée and me.

We're at Pembina Hills Sanatorium, down in the infirmary basement, inside a dimly lit conference room. Through a high small window that looks onto a snowy service road, I can just make out the tires of our car but not my stupid father. He's out of sight, not willing to help Maman, or us, face any of this.

I turn away from the window and back to the medical director, Dr. Grant. He's looking with watery blue eyes over his spectacles at Maman, and his words pierce through her little hope.

"There is no arbitrary six-month period to try to arrest this disease," he tells her. "Some patients are here much longer. That's why we call it chasing the cure. I need to be frank with you about this, Mrs. Côté."

Maman watches his lips move as she holds Josée on

her knee. With a free hand she touches Luc, slumped like an old man beside her, as if she'll never see him again.

Luc turns away angry eyes to hide his fear. I guess he and I are caught in the same thought: Oncle Gérard. For the first time in my life I'm actually scared for my brother. It's his thinness I now see, like a veil has been yanked back from my eyes. So much like Gérard, with the cough that seizes and shakes him. Not croup but TB!

I'd like to slap our local doctor. Why didn't he think, until Luc hemorrhaged from his lungs, to take a chest X-ray? And now here we are, all three of us. And our parents! Why didn't Maman, at least, stand up to Dr. McTavish and tell him to get Luc X-rayed months ago?

"Sometimes," Dr. Grant is saying, looking at Luc, "people surprise us and beat this disease against all odds. Whenever that happens, of course, it's a wonderful thing."

In the hallway Luc turns his head, holding me in a long last gaze from which I do not look away. In my own look I try to send him some courage. His bony fingers clutch the armrests of the wheelchair anyway, as if by doing this he can somehow bring everything, including this moment, to a stop.

But there's no stopping this. As he's being taken away to the east infirmary, Josée buries her face in Maman's neck and wails, "Noooo!"

Maman holds her tightly, until a nurse suddenly appears and lifts Josée out of her arms. Josée begins to scream, waving her arms at us as she, too, is taken away.

The nurse attempts clucking sounds of comfort, but of course we hear Josée's piercing cries all the way down the hall.

Maman's face twists into grief as I reach for her. I hold her in my arms as she holds me. Over her shoulder I look at Dr. Grant, who seems to be caught up in his own struggle, standing a little apart from us in the hallway.

Finally he says, "Come back into the conference room with me, Mrs. Côté, because there are a few more things I have to explain. And here's your wheelchair, Marie-Claire. Go with the nurse. Say goodbye to your mother for now. Visiting day is Sunday."

"I know it is," I say through choking tears. "I know it's Sunday."

He turns away, lowers his voice to my mother. "If you're worried about finances, that, at least, we can deal with. For the past couple of years the province has taken on paying for the care of all tuberculosis patients. And of course we also have . . . benefactors."

Just like that, on the word "benefactors," as if we are to be treated like charity cases, I am dismissed. Another nurse comes by and wheels me away. I swiftly swipe the tears from my eyes and sit up in my chair. I'm dying in my heart and I won't let her see this.

"The west infirmary is where you're going, and you'll be with another girl who is close to your age!" she says in falsely cheerful tones, as if all this matters to me.

The dark antiseptic smells of the institution fill my nose. I remember Oncle Gérard and the day I visited him. Now, here I am in this very same world of TB exiles. I'm one of them.

I'm wheeled into a room with two beds. One of the beds contains the roommate, whoever she is. I don't look at her.

Another nurse, whose name tag says Mrs. Thompson, helps me out of my clothes and into pajamas. She attaches a small brown paper bag with two safety pins to the mattress by the pillow. I start to cough.

She points to a covered waxed-cardboard cup and a box of tissues on the bedside table. "Spit in the cup—don't ever swallow your sputum—and cover your mouth when you cough. TB is an airborne disease."

"I know that, I'm not stupid," I mumble.

In my hand I'm still holding, like a small dead thing, the booklet I was given: *Welcome to Pembina Hills Sanatorium.*

Mrs. Thompson takes it from me, shuts it inside the drawer of the bedside stand, and says, "Rest. Don't sit up unless one of us helps you. Don't get out of bed for any reason. One of us will help you with the bedpan."

With a look that drills a hole into me to make sure I'm getting all of this, she says, "I'll be back later. To check up on you."

After that she leaves, her white shoes squeaking down the hall.

It's the second week of December 1941, and my world as a normal person has just ended.

"Hi," says the roommate from the pillows in the bed beside me.

I turn my head and finally take her in. She's very blond, almost white blond, her hair a cloud around a glittery-eyed, fevered, too-thin face—the face of TB.

"I hate this," I blurt out, and right away I wish I'd kept my thoughts to myself.

After a few seconds the girl says, "Nobody expects you to like it, but you'll get used to it, really you will."

On her smooth, pale hand, resting against white covers, is a ring that's beautiful and expensive looking. She's a rich city girl for sure. Those hands have never milked a cow.

I look down at my own red callused hands and hide them under the covers.

"I'm Signy Jonasson," she says suddenly.

"Marie-Claire Côté," I answer, not to be rude.

I turn over in the hard bed.

Dear Mother of God, just let me rest.

But the girl in the next bed has other plans. I hear her moving around under the sheets. Maybe she's trying to sit up on her own.

Finally she whispers, "I think it's fate that I found you

and you found me. I just know we're going to be wonder-ful friends!"

I think about this for a minute. I can feel her staring at my back, waiting.

What on earth would make her say such a crackpot thing—to me, a perfect stranger? I don't want to be friends. I want to sleep and never have to wake up to this night-mare.

A sickening shame has begun to creep over me. One that says it's as much my fault as anyone's that this has happened. I shouldn't have spent any more time than was necessary with Oncle Gérard after we found out he was sick. I should never have taken the train and put my brother in harm's way, or visited Gérard in his room here at the San, when he was red hot with TB.

That was just asking for trouble. And trouble is what we got.

SIX

At five o'clock they bring Signy Jonasson and me our evening meal: turkey soup, followed by turkey in white sauce with peas poured over a hot biscuit, and, for dessert, pears floating in thin syrup.

I test the pears first, putting a corner of the flesh into my mouth. I chew slowly, try to swallow, but it sits like a lump in my throat. Everything, it seems—even this pear, which normally would be a treat—makes me cry, and I don't want to.

I put down the spoon and pick up the knife and fork. They feel too heavy to hold. I drop them as well.

I look over at Signy Jonasson, who is slowly picking at her meal. She wants a conversation. I want to be left alone. I lift my knife and fork again and begin to force myself to eat so that I won't have to talk to her.

"They like it when you finish everything on your plate," Signy says.

I don't care to be spoken to in this manner. I'm not a child. And I don't care what "they" like or want, either.

"They're trying to build up our strength," she adds softly. "Is it in your lungs?"

What business is it of hers!

"You can get it anywhere in your body, but the lungs are the most common place to have it," she says, not bothering to wait for a reply. "So it's probably your lungs. Listen, Marie-Claire, I was at another sanatorium before this one. They had so many rules and the staff was mean and I hated it there. But it's nice here, really it is. You'll get used to it, I know you will, even a . . . shy person such as yourself."

Shy? I'm anything but shy! If I had the energy to throw a pillow at her, I'd do it.

"All kinds of interesting things happen," she goes on. "For instance, one of the nurses ran off with one of the patients, and when they got back two days later, they were married. Of course they can't live together—not yet—but the whole thing is so romantic."

Is she crazy? I can't imagine anything less romantic than the joining of two desperate people: one who is horribly sick, the other who looks after the horribly sick.

How the hell did I get stuck with this stupid girl?

Mrs. Thompson suddenly sails into the room, looks at our trays, and scowls.

"You girls are talking too much," she pronounces, "and now you're overexcited and can't eat. Honestly, you have to buckle down and take your cure seriously. Drink your milk, at least."

She folds her arms and stands over Signy, who slowly picks up her glass and downs her milk.

"Good girl," she says.

Turning to me, she comes over, lifts my wrist, and takes my pulse.

"Are you Luc Côté's sister?" she asks after a few seconds.

I stare her in the eyes, and if looks could kill, she'd drop dead on the floor in front of me.

She lays my hand once again on the covers. With that she leaves—disappearing like a phantom into the hall— leaving me to wonder why, exactly, she wants to know if I'm Luc's sister.

Around eight in the evening they bring us toast and tea and more milk, none of which I want. After that, wash- bowls. Then we brush our teeth. Somebody comes and gives us each a back rub with cold rubbing alcohol. Then we use the bedpans.

Right after, they bring out several sweaters and toques and half a dozen woolen bed socks.

"What's all this?" I say, turning to Signy.

She's busy. A new nurse, a brunette with fiery red lip- stick, is helping to pull a thick sweater over her head.

"You're going out on the balcony with the others, but first we'll Klondike you. You'll be tucked in all nice and snug," answers the red-lipped nurse, whose name is Miss Melnychuk. "Don't worry, it's part of the cure. We haven't lost a patient in the snow yet, trust me."

Trust her? I don't trust anybody in this place. But here's Red Lips, smiling over her shoulder like that's going to reassure me. I'm now thinking about Tante Angeline and how she said that San patients are shoved out in their beds onto the balconies even in thirty below zero weather. How I rolled my eyes at that one. But, apparently, it's true!

At home, you build up the fire in the woodstove and by morning the coals are dead. When your feet hit the floor, there's frost on the floorboards and a frozen-over washbasin to chink away at before splashing icy water on your face. But you haven't been lying all night out on the open prairie in the wind and the snow with killing temperatures! You wouldn't do that on a dare.

Red Lips, who is not going to spend the night outside, finishes with Signy, comes over, and calmly pulls me up and gets me ready to do that very thing.

"You should take my pulse," I blurt, my heart racing.

"We've already done that, honey," she coos, stopping to pat me.

I pull away. I'm not some baby to be comforted.

"Heart palpitations are normal in a TB patient," she continues cheerfully.

She stuffs me into a sweater, puts a toque on my head, and tugs it down over my ears. After that she pulls back the covers and goes to work on the bed socks. Shoves a hot water bottle somewhere near my feet.

Someone else has come into the room, a big man, tall as a giant, wild black hair. He jokes with Signy, as if what is about to happen is as normal as anything, and like they're old friends. All the while he keeps burying her in pillows and mounds of blankets flipped and tucked every which way. Only her eyes show as he's hauling her bed onto the balcony and the cold rushes in through the door.

"Don't run away," he calls out to me, like he's just said the funniest thing. "You're next."

Patients trapped in their beds. Pulled out of their warm rooms and onto a long frozen balcony. As for me, I can't turn onto my stomach like I'm used to doing. I'm stuck on my back, afraid to move, afraid of bringing frost inside the covers.

I miss having my warm little sister in bed beside me. I miss her soft breathing. Where is she tonight? What happens if she has to pee? What if she wets her bed? Who will hear and help her if she's crying and afraid?

The cold stars glitter in the dark, past the balcony screens. I remember Luc's face. The way he looked at me just before they took him away. I picture him in the same room, in the same bed where Gérard died.

But not Luc, he's tough! Right now, though, he's so sick

that maybe they'll keep him inside. I pray that's just what they'll do.

At last I think about the Virgin Mary. I think about her heart so pure, like fire. I ask her to please take care of Luc and Josée and me—even if she didn't manage to do so well with Oncle Gérard.

SEVEN

I wake up and I don't need a watch to tell me it's five in the morning. Then I remember that there aren't any cows to be milked, just a bunch of TB exiles lined up like cattle in this freezing barn of a balcony. My "hot" water bottle became useless hours ago. The pile of wool blankets that sits on top of me—especially heavy against my bladder—is not much use now, either.

I have to pee. I'm glad I said no to a drink of anything last night, or things would be worse.

Just when I think I might actually wet the bed for the first time since I was a kid, the bed-pullers finally arrive and haul us back to our rooms.

My eyelashes are frosted. Everything melts and slides down my face. The giant from last night introduces himself.

"William W. Samson. Middle double-U stands for wise guy, but you can call me Billy like everybody else. And how was that fresh air?"

I pierce him with a look. "If you really want to know, it was the worst night of my life!"

He tugs off my toque. Gives me his own evil look, which he seems to think is amusing, as I sink farther into my bed.

"Bah! You'll get so you love it! Have I ever lied to you?"

"So tell me the truth." I glare up at him. "Do we get shoved out into winter's wonders all the time?"

He thinks this over as he's getting me out from the trap of all my blankets. It seems no one in the history of this place has ever asked such a question.

With effort, he says at last, "Not if it's really cold."

"Really cold?"

"Really really cold. You know, cold."

He leaves. A nurse's aide comes by and then, thank God, it's a round of sitting on our bedpans. I wish there was some privacy, but I'm probably going to wish a lot of things that are useless to wish in a place like this.

Starchy Nurse Thompson bristles in, takes our temperatures and pulses, and records them. The first nurse's aide brings us washbasins and, soon after, another brings in breakfast trays—a small mound of porridge, toast, a perfect soft-boiled egg, juice, coffee, and milk.

Someone in the kitchen knows how to cook at least. I push the porridge aside anyway and start on the egg.

Signy's more flushed than yesterday. She eats half her breakfast. Suddenly, she throws everything up, all over herself and all over her bed. The room fills with the smell of vomit.

This brings back Mrs. Thompson.

"I'm so sorry!" Signy cries sickly.

She gasps for air. A deep rattling comes from her chest. The blankets come off, the sheets, a basin appears. My roommate is stripped and then washed with a tenderness that takes me by surprise, as Mrs. Thompson circles her chest and then her back with a soft white cloth.

But it's Signy herself who brands my brain: her naked body—she's thin as a skeleton, like Luc and Oncle Gé-rard, and a long angry scar runs down her back on the left side. Her shoulder droops and her ribs seem to have caved in. What's happened to her?

All at once I feel like throwing up, too.

A while later my tray is taken away. I'm given a bed bath.

Somebody else comes along with a mop and pail and washes the floor with strong-smelling carbolic soap. The room smells bad all over again. The radiator hisses rusty steam. This, too, smells bad.

There are the sounds: footsteps, voices up and down the hall, sounds of sickness from other patients in other rooms. Outside the winter wind picks up.

I long for the barn back home. I even long for our big cow, Jessie. Instead I'm stuck here, almost too tired to move. At least now I know it's TB that makes me feel this way.

Signy stares at the ceiling. I do the same. I stare at the same place she's looking at—a watermark shaped like a spider.

"A spider," I say, still in shock from breakfast.

"Sometimes, when the sun shines just right, it's a star."

I wonder how long she's been in this room. I hesitate, then ask, "How old are you?"

"Seventeen, this past October," she says, slowly turning her face on her pillow. "You?"

"Sixteen, almost. My birthday's on the twenty-first of this month."

And this is where I'll be on my birthday, I think. Stuck in this room. Stuck in this bed. Stuck with TB. Stuck with you.

"Oh," she says, perking up. "Winter solstice. In Iceland, where my grandparents come from, they throw a big party, kind of to welcome back the light."

"I never thought of it that way," I say glumly.

"What way did you think of it?"

"Too close to Christmas."

"Sweet sixteen," she says with a grin like a shrunken elf, "and never been kissed?"

What a stupid, nosy girl.

Marius Berard, when we were nine, caught me in the cloakroom one day after recess and kissed me in a slobbery way as he tried to put his hand up my skirt. I drew back and slapped him so hard I left a red mark on his face. Then he stumbled out from one side of the cloakroom and I marched out of the other.

I do not count that as a kiss. I count it as an insult.

No, I've only ever actually kissed Joe. When I write to

him next, I'm going to have to tell him I have TB. After he gets that letter, kissing is going to be the last thing he'll think of when he thinks of me. I wonder if you can get it from kissing a TB girl just once?

Signy looks back at the spider and says, "There was a boy who visited me sometimes when I was at that sanatorium in Winnipeg, but after I got here I didn't see him anymore. And then he went overseas. I still write to him. He's in the air force. His name is Sebastian. Would you like to see his picture?"

I could tell her yes, to be polite. It would be such a little thing. She's had a hard morning. But I don't want to see his picture. Or have a pathetic conversation about this boy. So I don't say anything.

She slowly rolls over onto her side anyway, opens the top drawer of her bedstand, pulls out a small photo, and rolls back with it to face me. The effort of doing this one thing leaves her out of breath. She reaches across, stretching her arm, her fingertips, as far as they'll go. I lean out of bed to help her by reaching even farther. The photo slips out of her hand. It flutters to the floor and lands face up.

Sebastian is very handsome. I can see this even from where I am, leaning over the side of the bed. He has the easy smile of a boy who's used to having as many girls as he pleases.

I start to get out of bed to pick it up.

"Don't," Signy warns. "What if they catch you?"

Just as my feet are about to touch the floor, in walks Mrs. Thompson.

I swing my legs around, shove them under the covers, and fall back in bed. The sudden movement makes me dizzy. I start to cough.

Mrs. Thompson leans down, picks up the photo, goes over and puts it inside Signy's bedstand. Then she comes back to me.

"Miss Côté," she says. "You have a TB lesion on your right lung. There's no pill on this earth that we can give you to fix that. There's no hope of us getting you better if you don't rest. That's the cure—besides eating properly and breathing in fresh air at night and during rest hours and, sometimes, surgery. Do I make myself clear?"

I shrink under the covers. What's a TB lesion? Will it kill me?

"Now, maybe you'd like to sit up for a while. You, too, Signy."

She fusses around, lifting us, smacking our pillows as if they are the enemy, arranging our blankets.

After she leaves, Signy says in a whisper, "At Christmas the nursing staff bring in cedar boughs and make garlands and string them up in the halls. The smell is divine, really it is. They decorate them with shiny glass balls and tinsel."

So she was here last Christmas—almost a year ago. And from the look of her, she isn't getting better.

EIGHT

A small bald man comes by with a mail cart. He grins at me, his teeth all yellow and crooked, and says, "So, you're the new one. Well, I've got no mail for you today, young lady. I've got an extra Eaton's catalogue though. If you can lift it, you can have it. The price is a smile."

He fishes it out from the bottom shelf of his cart. My life from now on, it seems, is going to be on display for everybody who comes through the door.

I don't smile. Instead I mumble, "Thanks."

He sets the catalogue beside me on the bed, backs his cart out of the room. Seconds later, the catalogue thuds to the floor.

"That was Frank Tate, and he's harmless, really he is," says Signy, to whom he has delivered a letter and two magazines, each one rolled up in brown paper. With delicate fingers she unfolds the letter, which I can plainly see is V-mail, probably from her airman. She wants to read it right now, I can tell, and I wish she'd just go ahead and do that.

Instead she lowers the letter and launches in. "Mr. Tate was a patient here for about ten years. Did you know that the medical director, Dr. Grant, once had TB, too?"

Dear God, doesn't anybody ever *leave* this place?

And do they all know each other's business? Might as well just put my bed right out on the main street of St. Felix for all the difference it would make. Everybody walking by, poking at me, saying good morning, while I sit on the commode with my bum in the breeze.

Five minutes later Dr. Louis Yuen, a tall, handsome Chinese guy, comes in and pulls up Signy's pajama top.

I am mortified for her. She, however, doesn't seem to be bothered. In fact this attention, stupid as it is, seems to please her!

She smiles—I can't imagine why—as Dr. Yuen listens to her deformed chest. Finally, he pulls her top down again and moves over to examine me.

"You're coughing quite a bit," he says, looking down at me. "You look quite flushed."

All business, he unhooks my chart from the end of the bed.

"Is your temperature up?"

I'm thinking, bugger off and don't you dare lift my top.

He does though, pressing the cold stethoscope here and there, asking me to breathe deeply. This makes me cough more.

"Spit," he says, indicating the sputum cup.

I pick up the cup, flip the lid, spit into it, and fall back against the pillows, my heart racing, my modesty shredded.

"How do you feel, Marie-Claire?"

"Like hell!" I snap.

He doesn't even flinch. Instead, he tucks my pajama top under the covers and says, "This is a tiring place. Not like home."

He stands back a bit and stares at me, long enough so that I start to feel uncomfortable. I don't know why he's staring or what he's thinking.

Then, "I saw your brother this morning. He said to say hello."

"Luc?"

"Yes."

I'm so relieved to hear from Luc, I start to cry in front of this white-coated man. If I'd been a good sister we never would've gotten on the train that day. I'd have taken him by the arm, hauled him back home, and kept him safe.

Dr. Yuen hands me a tissue. I take it from him, cough again, wipe my eyes, and blow my nose.

"He said, 'Say hello to Marie-Claire Côté, she's my big sister.'"

That's what Luc would say. That's just how he'd say it.

He stands there looking at me. Waiting for me to say the next thing. So I do.

"I want to know how he is." I raise my eyes to meet

Dr. Yuen's, daring him to tell me the truth. "How he really is."

He lowers his gaze to rest along my collarbone, and then his eyes come back to meet mine.

"He's in good hands, Marie-Claire," he offers with a tight smile.

Fear rises inside me like a hot flame. Fear for Luc— fear for us all, but especially for Luc.

"Does he . . . have a room by himself?"

"Oh no, we thought he'd like some company," he answers, relaxing. "He's in a room with three others. They're around your age—maybe a year or so older. I've asked them to keep an eye on him."

"Oh," I say, flooding with relief. At least now I don't have to imagine him all alone in a tiny room, like the one where Oncle Gérard died.

I press on. "And Josée, my little sister, I worried about her last night. I couldn't sleep. Who can sleep in all that cold!"

Dr. Yuen pulls up the chair and sits.

"Listen, you can't take care of her from your bed. Isn't that so?"

I lower my eyes.

"You have to leave that up to us, Marie-Claire. Am I right?"

"My sister is so little," I say at last to my folded hands.

"I saw her this morning, too. She was laughing."

I raise my eyes and snap, "Well, I'm not laughing! I

want to know what a TB lesion is! I want to know if TB will kill my brother and sister and me! Just when can we expect to drop dead—like Oncle Gérard!"

He's measuring me. I can almost feel his mind clicking, figuring what he should say next, how best to handle this crazy girl.

He puts out his hand. "May I?"

I nod, in tears once more, ashamed of my outburst, angry at feeling ashamed.

His hand comes to rest, high and light, on a spot on the right side of my chest, just under my collarbone. "A lesion is what your X-ray showed, what you have, there, inside your lung. It's a pocket made by your active TB—a cavity, so to speak."

He pulls his hand away.

A cavity? Does he mean that I have a hole in my lung? An actual hole?

I take in a breath. Let it out slowly. Begin to cough again.

"I knew your uncle, Gérard Côté. He was one of my patients, too. Nice guy, charming. Do you want to talk about him?"

I'm just so tired. I wish he'd go away. But there's something I have to ask him, even if I don't know how it's going to sound out loud. "Are you sure my uncle's the one who gave Luc TB?"

Dr. Yuen looks surprised. "What do you mean?"

I gulp down guilt and bile and still more shame. "One

time, I took my brother on the train to the San, and he . . . he caught a chill."

"A chill."

"Yes."

"You mean you think you're to blame for your brother's illness?"

I nod, hot tears swimming down my face.

"That's ridiculous," says Dr. Yuen.

I raise my eyes.

"Your brother slept in the same room with your tubercular uncle for several months, isn't that correct?"

I nod.

"In an enclosed space, hour after hour, week after week, month after month, and probably your uncle was coughing right into your brother's face as they slept, right?"

"That's true, but—"

"Your uncle lived a hard life. Quite possibly, he had TB for a long time without even knowing it. In the meantime, he passed his disease on to Luc. You and your sister were unlucky enough to get it, too."

"But I visited him, my uncle, here at the San when he was red hot with it."

Dr. Yuen sighs. "Look, I work here every day among the sick. Do I have TB? No, I don't. And we have large numbers of people working all over the institution— nurses, bed-pullers, lab and X-ray technicians, kitchen and laundry and powerhouse and carpentry and painting staff—and I can pretty much guarantee you, Marie-Claire, that not one of them has TB."

"Some of them have had it. So how come they got it?"

He gets up from the chair and retrieves the Eaton's catalogue from the floor. "Do you want this?"

I shake my head.

He stands there, sizing me up again. "Plainly speaking, TB loves an unhealthy body. If people are taking care of themselves, they're not likely to break down with it. Does that make sense?"

But we took care of ourselves, didn't we?

"This is going to take some time, Marie-Claire. You're aware of that, right?"

He puts the catalogue on the chair. "You're too keyed up. You have to settle down. Half the battle is making up your mind to fight this disease by lying low with it. I know that seems like a contradiction in terms, yet it's one of the things that actually works. I've seen it happen."

After he leaves, I suddenly feel like the stuffing's been knocked right out of me. Yesterday, a lifetime ago, when my brother and sister and I were admitted to this place, I was still trying to pretend that I wasn't really sick. Today my body is so much weaker. I can feel the TB moving in for a long visit.

Before long they come for us again, with toques, sweaters, bed socks. Wrapping us up inside the prisons of our beds. Hauling us back out onto the balcony for what they call "cure hour."

— ♥ —

I wake up, and this time remember where I am, turning my head inch by inch so as not to bring the winter air inside the covers. The sun's bright as a polished medal. Past the screens I see for the first time the tops of the burr oaks, gnarly branches all lumped with snow.

The cold air, I admit, makes my lungs feel good. I breathe in and out, willing it to attack the disease.

What if the cavity gets bigger? What will be left of my lung? My head hurts from worry. I wish I could stop thinking.

Frank Tate, the man who delivers the mail, finally appears and rescues us, bed wheels groaning over the floorboards. Inside, the hospital smells return.

I look over at Signy, pulling off her toque, smiling at me. I look away and think about her caved-in ribcage. How does she breathe on that side?

A ward aide takes our outside clothes and helps Signy into a quilted bed jacket made of green satin, lined in soft wool. A rich girl's jacket.

Next thing, I'm helped into a grayish brown wool cardigan of unknown origins—just as well, I don't think I want to know.

The ward aide leaves. Out of the blue, Signy says, "I guess I scared you this morning."

"I beg your pardon?"

"You probably need somebody to explain it, somebody

who's better at it than me. Maybe Dr. Yuen, when we see him again. He's so easy to talk to, isn't he? But for now . . . Well, first I had to have a pneumothorax. That's where they collapse the lung to make it rest."

"To make it rest?"

"Yes. So it has a chance to heal. Sometimes that doesn't work, though. I'd had pleurisy, you see, and there were all these painful adhesions sticking my lung to the chest wall. So then I had to have a thoracoplasty. That's where they cut out sections of your ribs—"

"They take them out?"

"Yes," she continues, cheerful as a bird, "usually seven or eight ribs. Well, in my case, nine. They didn't do it all at once. I had three operations. Anyway, my lung's collapsed for sure now."

She stops to catch her breath, quite literally. I roll back on the pillows, heart in my throat, mouth gone dry, and stare at the spider pattern on our ceiling.

Pneumothorax. Thoracoplasty.

What's going to happen to me? To Luc? To little Josée?

Mrs. Thompson comes and takes our temperatures and pulses, writes them on our charts. The lunch trolley trundles down the hall and stops by the door of our room. We are given our trays. Roast beef today, with gravy and mashed potatoes and peas and carrots and milk. Tomato juice. Apple cobbler.

It all smells delicious. Still I pick away at my food and choke down fear.

Signy slowly swirls gravy into her potatoes with her fork. "I went and upset you," she says, her mouth turned down at the corners. "You didn't want to hear all that stuff. I guess I talk too much."

Suddenly perking up again, she says, "TB isn't a death sentence, really it isn't. My friend Louise, who was in the bed that you're in now . . . well, she moved out to one of the cottages on the grounds. I just know that before long she'll be going over to the dining hall in the main building for one meal a day, and then she'll be allowed to take long walks, and after that they'll start to talk about a work-up program for her."

I don't want to hear about her stupid friend and her pathetic progress in this stupid pathetic place.

Just try to eat, I think to myself. Don't listen to her.

Shut your ears. Bite your tongue.

NINE

All during week one my fever goes up. My fever goes down. My fever goes up again. I cough and cough. I shiver and sweat. I feel nauseous and it's hard to eat.

Signy doesn't cough. I finally ask her why, seeing as how she's been here so long.

"The thoracoplasty stopped it . . ." She looks over at me with big eyes and shuts up.

Thoracoplasty hangs around the room anyway, the unwelcome guest that never leaves.

The librarian comes by with his cart. He's an ancient man named Reginald Sweet, who wears a suit that looks like it's been with him since the last war.

I'm glad to see him, though. Back home, I read whenever I could.

"Oh, that Marie-Claire, she's always reading," Maman said with pride one day to Tante Angeline. Maman, who used to be a teacher before she married Papa.

Tante Angeline, suspicious of anyone who has been to high school, sniffed and said, "She'll ruin her eyes. Next thing she'll need glasses. That's what comes from reading. And another thing—she'll get ideas."

I've read just about every title in our own parish library in St. Felix, even the boring ones, and believe me, there are several boring ones. So I'm not exactly sure what ideas I'm supposed to be getting.

I choose a novel, *Anna Karenina*, by Leo Tolstoy, noting happily that it's thick with pages. The soft navy-blue cover has been worn ragged by many hands.

Soon as it's in my hands, though, I find it's too heavy and I'm too weak to hold it up.

Signy's chosen a book with fewer pages, *Tuberculosis and Genius*.

I try to prop my book with my knees. It's useless. I'm too damn weak to even hold up a book. But I don't return it.

The librarian says, "Give it time, young lady. Time's your friend here."

He bends over his cart and totters out of the room.

"Always the philosopher," says Signy, flipping through her own book. "Did you know that Jane Austen had TB? Says so right here. Also the Brontë sisters, Voltaire, Robert Louis Stevenson, the poet John Keats. A whole bunch of geniuses."

Geniuses? Does this mean I can expect to become a genius because I have TB? What will she think of next?

She puts down the book. She's been here so long that she's probably read everything in the library a thousand times.

"I read *Gone with the Wind* and *Anna Karenina* last year," she says. "Before I had the stuff leading up to my, you know . . ."

Thoracoplasty—how could I forget, since she won't let me.

Every day she listens to her radio. One of her favorite programs is *The Shut-ins Show*, where they dedicate songs to patients in sanatoriums and hospitals across the province. The announcer tries hard to cheer on all us "shut-ins," but his sickbed tones are a pain. Sometimes, though, he plays good music.

On Saturday night, at the end of my first week at Pembina Hills, we're listening to Tommy Dorsey's band.

Signy, who writes a lot more letters than she gets, is composing another one, probably to her airman.

I'm trying to get up the energy to write a few lines to Joe. Only I can't think of how to tell him about my TB. I lift my pen and write, *Dear Joe, how are you?*

Now what do I say? *I've been exiled to a TB san and I have a big hole in my lung . . .*

Signy romantically lifts her pen and finishes another line.

Suddenly the announcer comes on again. "This next one is going out to a certain little French charmer at Pembina Hills San, from a fellow sufferer."

I turn my head in shock, just in time to catch a smile from Signy, whose pen hovers over the page.

The Andrews Sisters come booming over the airwaves singing their big hit song "Boogie Woogie Bugle Boy."

They're beautiful girls—Maxene, Patty, and LaVerne—with beautiful voices. Their harmony goes right through me and gives me goose bumps.

After the song there's dead air, then the hissing and popping of static. I picture the Andrews Sisters off somewhere entertaining the troops while I'm stuck in this bed with TB.

Who will dance with me now? I can't even imagine it.

Signy puts down her pen. "I only wanted to surprise you," she says, sounding disappointed.

What does she expect? I can't say anything. My stupid, angry tears won't allow it.

I pick up my pen, rub my eyes, and start again. If I can't think of what to say to Joe other than the obvious, then I can damn well write that. So I do. When I'm done, my words on the V-mail take up barely a page. But at least I've told him now. At least I've done that.

On Sunday morning, Dr. Yuen, who never seems to sleep, lifts his eyes from my chart.

"You're not coughing as much. So you've decided to settle down, have you?"

"I'm resting," I inform him, "between battles."

It's true I'm not coughing as much. Perhaps it's the

endless hours of just lying here. Dear God, if the TB doesn't kill me, the boredom will.

"You seem kind of blue." Dr. Yuen's eyes are back on the chart. "And you've been here only—let me see—onetwothreefour . . . right, six. Six days. Right?"

He looks at me again.

I could tell him to go to hell. But I don't.

"Marie-Claire," he continues, in a patient tone that grates on me, "this is not such a terrible place. We don't beat you. In fact we make a big fuss over you. Isn't that right?"

Seeing as how he's humoring me, I'll ask him a question.

"Dr. Yuen, I need to get . . . some notes—to my brother and sister."

"Notes." Eyes on the chart again. "Depends on how many. Nervous energy is exhausting. I want you resting."

"Just a couple, and then I won't move. I promise."

I'll lie here for goddamn days, waiting for that fat spider up on the ceiling there to come down and make cobwebs all over me.

I write to Josée: *I'm sending you kisses and congratulations for being a brave girl! Oceans of love, Marie-Claire.*

I pause and consider crossing out the word "congratulations." Maybe it's too big for her. But then I leave it. She'll understand it means something good.

Then I write to Luc: *I'm in room 24, west infirmary. How are you? Let me know.* I pause, lick the end of my pencil, and write what's really on my mind. *I'm sorry I made you sick that time. Write me back. Please. Marie-Claire.*

In the afternoon, Dr. Yuen surprises me with a note from Luc—surprising especially since it's not in his handwriting. *room 31, east infirmary. What time? But can you help me remember about my tin with all my nickels and pennies that I was saving because I try and I try and I can't remember where I put it. Somebody might steal it. Luc.*

And written under that: *Dear Marie-Claire, I'm one of your brother's roommates. He's a tough kid, just not feeling so hot today, so I'm being his secretary. Hope you don't mind. Yours truly, Jack Hawkings.*

I guess Luc doesn't blame his TB on a train ride with his crazy sister after all. I quickly write: *Nobody's going to steal it, Luc, I promise—cross my heart! Just close your eyes and fly back home in your mind and soon you'll see where you put that tin. I'm sending you a big hug even though I know you hate them. Your big sister, Marie-Claire.*

After that another quick note: *Dear Jack, can you let me know if there's anything else he needs, please? I'm so worried about him. Yours truly, Marie-Claire Côté.*

Close to suppertime I get another note: *Luc says to tell you that he all of a sudden remembered! This is a big relief to all of us here in room 31. It was getting to be something of an obsession. Now he wants me to tell you that he's always wanted to fly and when he gets out of this place he's going to join the Royal Canadian Air Force! And now he's telling me to sign off, "with my compliments, your brother Luc." Bossy little beggar. Told you he's got lots of fight in him. Yours truly, Jack Hawkings.*

"No more notes," says Dr. Yuen, hands in the gaping pockets of his white ward coat. "You've cheered up your brother, though. Good for you."

If he's so "cheered up," why can't he write his own notes? It's too late to ask Dr. Yuen, who is already out the door, his white coattails flying behind him.

I keep the notes. I press them like flowers in the middle of my *Welcome to Pembina Hills Sanatorium* booklet, in the drawer of my bedside table.

Sunday afternoon Maman comes to visit, looking worried, all wrapped up in Grand-mère's fur coat, her rubber galoshes unzipped and flapping at her ankles.

"So where is he?" I ask, rising on my elbows, trying to see around her, trying to see if maybe Papa's just slowly coming up the hall and hasn't arrived yet.

"He's out in the car."

"Oh, of course," I say, sinking back. "Hiding away in a snowbank, as usual."

She smiles a little and perches like a stranger on the edge of my bed.

"You look rested," she says.

"Of course I look rested! How else would I look?"

"Oh my dear," she says, as tears start to roll down her cheeks.

Suddenly she gathers me up from my pillows and into her arms. I love the smell of her. I never want her to let me go.

"Be careful," warns Nurse Thompson, leaving the room. "She's very weak."

Maman releases me, looking as if she's been slapped.

I catch my breath. "Maman, I want out of this place! I hate it here!"

"I'm sorry about Papa," she whispers.

"He's a damn coward."

"Ah, Marie-Claire," she says, "don't be like that."

"He blames me, doesn't he?"

"What?" says Maman with a startled look.

"Papa. For this mess we're in. He thinks it's my fault."

"Nobody is blaming anybody," Maman says quickly. "And I have to go now, and you have to be a good girl. Do what the doctors say, so you can get well. Please promise me that."

"I don't want to be good." I fold my arms across my chest. "Maybe I'll take up smoking and drinking like Oncle Gérard."

She gets up from the side of the bed. "I have two other children to visit," she tells me softly.

"I know that," I pout. "You don't need to remind me. You get to visit them, and I don't."

She gives me her hand then and stands for a long while looking down at me, as if she wants to tell me something, but thinks better of it.

Finally, with a shake of her head and a parting squeeze of my hand, she says, "*Je t'aime, Marie-Claire, je t'aime.* I'll tell Luc you said hello."

After that she leaves.

If she'd said both their names, both Luc and Josée, I wouldn't have thought more about it. But it's just Luc. *I'll tell Luc you said hello.*

I think about that, then about how somebody else had to write those notes for him. And now I've got a funny feeling in my stomach, one that says no matter what, no matter who I have to get past, I have to go to him.

TEN

It's Monday morning, at the beginning of my second week.

Mrs. Thompson folds her arms across her chest and says, "What were you thinking, trying to get out of bed?"

I got as far as the hallway before my legs gave out. Billy Samson brought me back to my room. Now I'm in bed again, panting, coughing, sweating, and swimming with nausea.

Mrs. Thompson suddenly lifts me to sit, says, "Don't choke," and sticks a kidney basin under my chin. I heave up breakfast.

She cleans me up and sets me back on the pillows. I turn onto my side so she can't see my face. Signy looks at me, then over my shoulder at Mrs. Thompson and says, "She's worried about her brother, Luc."

"I know. I know who he is."

"I think she was trying to go and see him."

"That's not a good idea, Marie-Claire. Your temperature is up quite a bit today. In fact I've asked Dr. Grant to take a look at you."

She leaves. About half an hour later Billy Samson brings a wheelchair to my bed and says, "I'm taking you to X-ray, okay, kid?"

"Why do I need another X-ray? Why can't I just sleep?"

"You can sleep later," he says, helping me into the chair. "I'll personally see to it you get back here in one piece, how's that?"

Signy suddenly reaches out her hand. I don't know what to do except just reach out and take it. It's soft and warm, as light as bird bones.

"It'll be an adventure," Signy whispers. "Think of it as a trip to a foreign land. And don't stop breathing unless they tell you to."

I start to laugh—a little hysterically—but it's good to laugh. Billy wheels me through the echoing corridors down to the X-ray lab. Shortly after, Dr. Grant and Dr. Yuen frown and nod at my plates and make humming sounds of agreement and smile reassuringly at me.

Dr. Grant says, "I'll come down to the ward soon."

I'm sent, not at all reassured, back to my room.

A bit later, Dr. Grant comes to see me. The effort of going to X-ray has given me more than the usual heart flutters. I can't stop coughing.

"Your cavity has grown," he says, putting a hand on

my shoulder. "We need to rest that lung. What do you say, Marie-Claire?"

Oh God, will they take out my ribs?

"Dr. Yuen will perform the procedure," Dr. Grant adds.

My heart falls to my feet.

"It's called a pneumothorax," he continues. "He's just going to put some air through a needle between your ribs, into the pleural cavity that surrounds your right lung, the one with the cavity. After that—every week or so—you'll be given more air to keep that lung collapsed and resting."

No ribs cut. Yet the thought of pneumothorax is terrifying. How painful will it be? And how will I be able to keep breathing with just one lung? But then, Signy has a collapsed lung—with nine ribs removed besides—and she's still breathing.

I look over at her. She's turned onto her side, facing me.

If she can be brave, so can I.

Still, I don't feel one bit brave. Not at all.

I've been rolled onto my side. I want to keep breathing from both lungs for as long as possible.

Stalling for time, I say, "Tell me again, why do we have to rest it?"

Dr. Yuen, behind me, answers, "We hope that this will help to keep your TB from spreading. I'm using a little novocaine. Do you know what that is?"

"Anesthetic?"

Before I can think of what to say next, there's a prick of cold on my skin. Right after, a blunt force pushing between my ribs. Another few seconds, and then nothing.

I wait. Still nothing.

"Okay, Marie-Claire?"

I can't speak for the shock of feeling this nothing. Shouldn't I be feeling something dramatic by now?

"Just a few more cc's of air and we're done," he says.

"I'm breathing, somehow," I tell him.

Just as I say this, I'm aware of it—of the dead calm on my right side.

"Remember that you have full use of your left lung," Dr. Yuen says. "It's going to do all the work for now."

Back in our room, Signy, writing another letter, lifts her head. This time it isn't Billy who has brought me back. It's another orderly, one who yawns just before he bangs my foot on the doorframe.

I am too concentrated on my newly collapsed lung to notice this very much.

Mrs. Thompson bustles into the room behind us and says, "Mr. McFadden, this is not how we do things around here!"

"Sorry," he says with a sleepy shrug to me, as he prepares to haul me out of the wheelchair.

"You are needed down in room 27," she snaps.

"Now?"

She glares at him as he leaves.

"Honestly, what a damn fool," she mutters, easing me back into bed.

I want to ask her how I can possibly expect my left lung to do all the work. Now I want and need Maman.

Mrs. Thompson's eyes come into focus—the peaked white nurse's cap, the short gray hair fluffed around it, her wrinkling skin. She covers me, briskly tucks me in all around, and hurries away from my bedside.

I listen to the quiet in the room, to Signy's pen scratching across her notepaper, to my thudding heart, and then this, too, falls away as I become aware of breath moving into, and moving out of, my valiant left lung.

ELEVEN

I doze, in and out of the world. I have no appetite. They move me back and forth, into and out of the winter air. I lose track of time.

At one point I wake up and Maman is in the room sitting beside me.

I ask, "Is it Sunday?"

"No, it's Wednesday," she says, taking my hand, stroking it. "Go to sleep, Marie-Claire. Just rest."

By Friday, I'm starting, in a kind of feeble way, to sit up in bed again. Mrs. Thompson appears, rearranges my blankets, and says, "You have a visitor."

It's not visiting day. Maman, I think.

But it isn't Maman. I hear the sound that the skirts of the nuns make as they walk down the halls at school. Next thing, Sister Thérèse is in the room, filling it with her height and her disapproval.

She's brought me an orange. She holds it out to me before she sits.

"Thanks," I say, meekly setting it on my bedside table.

She finally takes a chair, scraping it across the floor like chalk across a blackboard. At last she sits, primly tucking her hands up inside the front panel of her habit.

Then she speaks.

"Well, I never expected to be visiting my star pupil in a place like this." She sniffs, glancing up at the ceiling, at the spider pattern. "Somebody forgot to clean up there."

"It's okay," I tell her softly.

She flashes me an angry look. "What's okay? That you and your brother and sister are all in this place?"

"No," I say, and then, "No," again, because she always tongue-ties me.

"Of course, it's no surprise. You were underweight and overworked."

At this, she indignantly pulls her hands out from her habit, picks up the orange from my table, peels it, slaps it into my open palm, and says, "For the love of God, eat this. You're fading away in front of us."

I obey her. She never gives you much choice in the matter. I slowly eat while she watches.

Before she leaves, she pulls something else from her pocket—a brand-new rosary. "You probably forgot to bring one with you, didn't you."

A statement, not a question. I have never been as pious as Sister Thérèse would like me to be.

I take the rosary anyway. "I . . . I guess so."

"Either you did or you didn't."

When I don't say anything, she says, "You're a proud, stubborn girl, Marie-Claire. And pride is a sin. It will trip you and thwart you and put lies on your tongue. You have a rosary now. Use it. The Holy Mother is always listening."

In my heart of hearts, I've always wanted a sixteenth birthday party. Yet even though it falls on an apparently special day, winter solstice, I'm not holding my breath—no pun intended.

Sunday again. Six days after my pneumothorax, the great day has at last arrived, finding Signy, the rich city girl, and me, the poor country girl, sitting, as usual, on bedpans.

TB, I'm beginning to discover, is a democratic kind of disease. The only requirement seems to be that you have lungs.

Then, right after breakfast, Signy reaches into her bedside table, pulls out a little wrapped box, and weakly tosses it over to me.

It's pink. The tissue paper fluffed up to resemble a rose. Tied with a generous length of thin blue satin ribbon.

"Happy birthday," she says breathlessly. "I've been counting the days."

"But . . . how . . . ?"

"My mum—she doesn't mind shopping."

Signy gets lots of packages from her mother in the city.

Only yesterday she received three magazines and a brand-new bed jacket.

I carefully remove the wrapping, smooth the lovely paper. Stop to tie my hair back with the ribbon. Then I lift the top of the box.

A ring sparkles up at me—gold, with a pearl at its center!

I close the box quickly. I can't believe what I've just seen. I open the box again. It's still there. I didn't imagine it.

Signy says, "Every girl should get something pretty on her sixteenth birthday, don't you think?"

Then she's quiet as I try it on.

The ring fits perfectly. I don't know how she managed this. But as I stare down at it, it starts to make my hand look strange. Like some other girl's hand, not my own. And it's too much—such an extravagant gift, from someone I barely know.

"C'est jolie, Signy," I tell her shyly, because it is pretty.

"Oh, I'm so glad!" she gushes. "I hoped you'd like it. Marie-Claire, I've been so very worried about you. But I don't want to make you feel uncomfortable about this, okay? It's just that . . . well, maybe this'll remind you of what's waiting when you get better. When we both . . . get better. Something, or somebody . . ."

She turns her head away. Looks out the window. Snow, snow, and more snow.

"Maybe," she says softly, "we'll get dressed up and

go to lunch together at some restaurant. We'll sit at a table with flowers. And flirt with the waiter."

I've never been to a restaurant. Or met a waiter. Or been to the city. Or gone to lunch. How in the world could I ever explain that to someone like her?

"That would be nice," I tell her, not knowing what else to say.

I leave the ring on my hand for about an hour. But it stings my pride to wear it and, as secretly as I can, I slip it back into the box.

Signy catches me just as I'm sliding the box into my bedside table.

It was bound to happen anyway. Soon enough she would have noticed I wasn't wearing the ring.

"I don't want to lose it, of course," I lie quickly. "Your mother must have paid a lot of money for it."

"Not so much."

She rolls over in bed, turning her back to me.

"Really, she didn't," she adds softly, after a while.

Right before morning cure hour, our village priest, Father Boulanger, comes to see me. He sinks, as if completely exhausted, into the chair beside my bed. His thick spectacles are smeared. He squints at a snapshot he holds in his hand, as if he's trying to see something there that he's missed. When he hands the photo to me—it's crinkled and cracked—it sits like a dry leaf in my hand.

"Take it, it's yours. Happy birthday, Marie-Claire," he

says solemnly. "Cadeau will now smile at you from your bedside."

Cadeau doesn't smile. I can only remember his scowls and snarls—a large brown dog who growls at everyone in our village and who loves only Father Boulanger.

Yet I'm happy with this nutty present that says my world is still out there   my own world, if only I can get it back. I tell Father Boulanger thank you and, at that, he gets up without another word and leaves, not even asking me to make confession!

In the afternoon Maman visits—just Maman. My heart sinks as she sits, placing a gift on the covers. I open it and it's a blue bed jacket, which Maman must have knit herself. It's very pretty, but I don't put it on. I leave it draped across my knees on the bed covers as I mumble, "Thanks."

Of course Papa blames me for what has happened to us. Why else would he choose not even to come by to see me on my birthday!

Maman's looking at her hands. At last she says, "Marie-Claire, I know what you're thinking, but Papa is here. He's just . . . he's with Luc . . ."

Her voice breaks. And then I know.

She raises her eyes, struggles to go on, and can't seem to. She quickly reaches out and takes my hand. Fear leaps around inside my heart.

"Josée is doing very well," she whispers.

"But Luc? Tell me what's happening—Maman?"

"This wasn't the news I wanted to bring to you," she says, holding me in a hard grip.

"I have to see him. When can I see him?"

They won't let me do this, Maman says. Apparently I'm too sick. It would make things worse.

Is she crazy? How could things get any worse? Maman leaves me in tears to go and see Luc.

Mrs. Thompson is working nights now, and Red Lips—Miss Melnychuk—is back on days. I swipe away my tears as she comes by.

"Please," I say to her, "I need to see my brother. He's very, very sick."

Her crimson mouth twists in surprise.

"I went to X-ray the other day in a wheelchair," I plead. "Couldn't somebody take me to see him in his room? I wouldn't stay long. I promise. I have to see him."

She looks at her watch, as if this will give her the answer, and mutters, "Yuen's on call."

Twenty minutes later Dr. Yuen shows up looking sleepy, like he's just woken from a nap.

"What's this about, Marie-Claire?"

"I need to see Luc."

He looks at me, then at Signy, who appears to be holding her breath, then at Red Lips, who's leaning against the door, arms folded, examining her white shoes.

"I don't think that's a good idea, Marie-Claire," he says quietly.

"Yes, it is," I say, starting to sob. "It's a very good idea."

Silence.

Then I'm angry. "Don't you think I know what's going on?" I explode. "And there's nothing I can do about it except . . ."

I begin to wail. Suddenly I'm gasping for breath.

Dr. Yuen says something softly to Red Lips, and she quickly leaves the room.

Next thing, she's back with a syringe.

I put out my hand, try to calm myself. She comes over, begins to roll up my sleeve, and a cold resolve comes over me.

"No," I say. "I don't want that."

She stands back, looks at me, then at Dr. Yuen. He hasn't taken his eyes off me.

"What I want," I say, "is to see my brother."

Dr. Yuen turns his face away, and I count several seconds.

"Could you go and get her a wheelchair, please?" he says to Red Lips at last.

"Is that—?"

"A good idea?" he finishes for her. "Apparently, yes. I'll take her there myself."

She goes and gets the wheelchair. He awkwardly helps me into it. I sit up straight. I try to calm myself by taking long, deep breaths in my good lung, the one that has not failed me, as we go along, through the halls, past patient rooms and offices, the lab, the X-ray, the conference room, to a set of elevators in the east infirmary. We get into a rattling cage with doors that clank shut, and then we move in short jerks up to the third floor.

Dr. Yuen pushes me smoothly down the long hall. We reach a door and enter Luc's room.

Everyone is standing around him—Papa, Maman, and Father Boulanger.

My brother is so small in his bed. He seems to have shrunk in just two weeks. It hurts to look at him.

His three roommates are playing a quiet game of cards, or doing something like that with their hands. They glance up, then respectfully away, as my own useless hands begin to tremble in my lap.

Dr. Yuen brings me closer to Luc, reaches over and moves a few things out of the way, then pushes me closer still, so that I'm right up beside him.

Maman and Papa are weeping quietly. Father Boulanger is praying, his voice just a whisper.

Luc seems somehow younger than his eleven years, against his pillows, his eyes closed. His arms, his hands, rest outside the covers. He doesn't even look like himself.

Yet when I take his cold hand, I feel that he's still my brother. He's still in there somewhere, dreaming. I feel as if I'm in a kind of dream, too, as I start to talk to him. I tell him that I'm proud to have him as my brother, and that I'm sorry for all the times I ignored him or got mad at him. And then I settle in to telling him things, the way you do when you start to remember.

Before long it's an unstoppable rush, like when winter melts and runs through the ravine back home every spring. When we were kids, remember, Luc? The geese flying in a V over our heads, and the purple crocuses coming back and covering the hills? And the smell of it, that smell of spring, and laughing and running and getting soaked in the rain? The time you helped me rescue the calf that got caught in the barbed wire, remember that? It was calling for its mother and she was calling for it and neither of them stopped calling until we freed it? And then remember us sitting out in that old abandoned car in the bush, with the leaves falling all around us that day . . .

I finally stop, only because Luc's hand has twitched inside mine and I feel the life in it. Maybe inside himself he's remembering those things, too.

The priest has stopped praying. Maman and Papa have stopped crying. Dr. Yuen is saying, "It's time to go, Marie-Claire."

One of Luc's roommates, a tall guy who is a little older than me, stands, shoulders hunched, by the door.

"I'm Jack," he says. "I'm real sorry . . ."

But Dr. Yuen is already pushing me into the hall. He wheels me quickly to the elevator and all the way back to my room without saying a single word. And I'm grateful not to have to talk.

— ♥ —

Out on the balcony during the long night, I listen to the winter wind and pray. I want a miracle. The rosary from Sister Thérèse is in my hands, under the covers. I fall asleep, wake with a start, say my rosary, fall over the edge of sleep again.

At last, when it's morning, I feel calmer—as if anything could happen. Maybe God has heard me. The lights come on and cut through the darkness of December. A light in one of the rooms, somewhere in this big building, I know, burns bright for Luc.

The slow march of beds back to our own rooms begins. Billy Samson, the resident giant, comes for me. This morning I'm glad to see him.

"Hi, Billy." My breath hangs in clouds around me.

"Good morning, there, little snowman." He looks down at me with solemn eyes.

"And how are you?" I ask encouragingly. Does he know something I don't?

I try to push away the picture that's growing inside my head. My brother taking in small breaths, mouth opening and closing like a bird knocked from its nest.

Billy pulls my bed through the door. It bumps lightly back into the infirmary.

He knows something, for sure. He's different this morning, not as hearty as usual. Still he smiles at the sight of Signy—her toque pulled off, her pale blond hair standing up wildly with static electricity from the dry cold.

After he leaves Signy says, "I prayed for your brother last night. Lutheran style."

I want to be left alone with my prayers for Luc. I don't want to know that she's been praying, too. Just in case, though, I turn away and send up another prayer that maybe between the Catholics and the Lutherans we can pull him through.

Yet dread piles heavily against my heart. Just before breakfast, Father Boulanger, his long robes flowing black, comes into the room, followed by Maman—and Papa.

This is how I know it has happened.

Papa can barely walk. Maman's face is wretched with tears. They hold on to each other, hold each other up. I struggle to sit up in bed and watch them move like shadows toward me.

TWELVE

God must be deaf this Christmas. I can't even go to my own brother's funeral. How is it that life can be so cruel? Maman and Papa disappear to make the arrangements I can't stand to think about.

Cedar garlands suddenly show up in the infirmary halls. One is even hung across the ceiling of our room. I watch as Mrs. Thompson dangles red and blue and silver balls from it, decorates it with tinsel. She moves more slowly than usual, with small looks my way.

In fact everyone creeps around me like shadows. I breathe in. I breathe out. Hours go by with their rounds of bedpans and bed baths and meals and rest in the winter air. I don't speak. I've lost my heart, my hope.

I can't imagine Luc anywhere. Did God take him to a nice place? How, with all that he suffered, could he end up in a bad place? And what of Baby Jesus? How can it be, on His happiest of holiest of days, that I'm brotherless?

Back home on Christmas Eve we would be getting ready to go to midnight mass. Maman's tourtière warming on top of the woodstove for the feast afterward. Luc slicking down his hair with water, combing over that stubborn piece that would never sit flat. Pulling his brown sweater over his white shirt. Slipping a small toy into his pocket so he could play with it behind Maman's back during mass when he was bored. Josée in her frilly white blouse and little shoes. Maman in her good dress, with the brooch Papa gave her as a wedding gift so many years ago. People streaming to the church in cars and trucks and horse-drawn sleighs. Voices in harmony, the beautiful Christmas songs.

I weep for the fact that we'll never, as a family, hear them again.

Christmas Eve on the ward. Signy's parents arrive straight from the train, an eight-hour ride across the prairies from Winnipeg. It seems that even the rich can't come by gasoline for their cars these days. Mr. Jonasson has a dark mustache, like Papa's. Mrs. Jonasson wears a fur coat and a fur hat over her reddish blond hair.

"Marie-Claire," Signy says, "this is my mum and dad."

Her father smiles gravely and offers me his beautifully manicured hand. I take it, and it surrounds mine. Her mother, smelling of rich perfume, pulls off leather gloves and takes both my hands in her satiny grip.

"Signy told us about your brother. We're so very sorry for your loss, Marie-Claire, so, so sorry."

I don't know what to say, so I don't say anything. She's kind and motherly. But she isn't Maman. Where is Maman tonight? Where is Papa? Are they weeping at home? Will they go to mass?

I hear music in the hall coming toward us. Voices singing "Silent Night." Musicians with their instruments appear at our door—a fiddle, a saxophone, a guitar, and an upright piano rolled along on its wheels. Then everyone tries to crowd into our room—the carolers, maybe twenty or so, along with the musicians. Those who can't make it into the room crush together in the hall by the door.

"This is what they do for us every Christmas," Signy says to her parents and me. "This is what we wait for."

Just then the crowd parts. In walks Dr. Yuen. He's dressed as Santa Claus and pushing a wheelchair. In the chair, looking lost and alarmed by all this noise, wearing pink slippers on her little feet, is my sister, Josée!

Someone lifts her up. Puts her on my bed. She leans against me. She turns up big frightened eyes to take in my face—at first, as if I'm a stranger.

Suddenly she lifts her hand, pats my cheek. "Is it you, Marie-Claire?"

I can't find my voice. Instead, I hug her close, breathing her in.

Who Will Love Me?

Spring 1942

THIRTEEN

May, May, the merry month of May.

I'm not sure who is merry.

Rest, rest, rest, rest, rest, rest, rest.

And more rest.

Five months of resting. Five months of staring at walls. Staring past frozen screens. Staring at each other. Crying, sometimes in secret and sometimes not. Lifted. Poked. Reassured, then poked again.

Signy and I have at last been given bathroom privileges (which counts as our "exercise"). And, just recently, we're allowed to take a bath alone, in an actual tub. The bath happens once a week.

This morning, my bath day, I wrap an ugly chenille dressing gown around my pajamas, drop a bar of lily-of-the-valley bath soap into one saggy pocket and some scissors and a bottle of Breck shampoo—for that halo of beauty—into the other. I shuffle into the corridor just as an orderly comes out of the room across the hall.

He pushes a gurney, and on it somebody who is covered head to toe in white. Actually not some body—or just any *body*. It's Mrs. Haliday, a woman with a husband and five children.

The orderly pretends he doesn't see me, as he rolls the stretcher past. It rumbles along to the back elevator that will take her down to the morgue.

Another casualty of TB.

Who will be in her bed next?

I would pray for her soul, but I've given up on God—the Father and the Son—and all the deaf saints and, especially, Mary, Mother of God, who seems to have given up on her children here on earth.

I go into the bathroom and draw a hot bath. We've been told that we're only supposed to go through the effort of washing our hair once a month. But I'm sick of living with greasy hair.

I look at my thin face in the bathroom mirror. My brown eyes like Luc's, my curly hair like Luc's.

I put the blades of the scissors about four inches from my scalp—it'll be easier to take care of this way—and start to chop. I toss each section in the wire basket by the sink.

I lean into the mirror again. Now I really do see my brother. He's there just under the surface of my own dead stare.

I climb into the tub, hold my breath, my nose. Plunge backward in the water. Very fast I'm up, clutching at the sides of the tub. Gasping for air from my lung that works.

I apply shampoo. My hands are weak. I scrub until I no longer can. I rub soap over my body and cry, poor me, boohoo—a long ugly cry.

Rinse everything off. Wobble out of the tub. Wipe myself down, throw dirty pajamas into the laundry basket, pull fresh pajamas from the shelf, and stagger into them.

Now back to my room. Sixty-seven steps.

Finally I fall back into bed.

Signy turns her head and stares at me.

"What?" I turn my face to her.

I'm sweating from my efforts, heart still pounding.

"You look like a movie star." She points to a picture in one of her movie magazines. "See?"

"I can't see," I tell her irritably. "You're over there and I'm over here."

"I knew you were going to cut your hair," she says, nose back in the magazine. "I saw you sneak those scissors into your pocket. Next thing we'll have boys under our balcony whistling at you."

Sometimes she says the most peculiar things. I keep staring at her—at her tired face, tired as mine—and can't imagine what would make her think about boys under our balcony.

Or what we'd do with them!

Of course, there are boys. East infirmary boys, yes,

and then the ambulant males in the cottages and other buildings on the sanatorium grounds—young guys struck down by TB, too sick to go to war. We see them, with their hands shoved in the pockets of their spring jackets, walking like ghosts up and down the road beyond the lawn and the trees. After meals in the dining hall, this is where they take their exercise.

These are the only hints that Signy and I have of the possibility of romance. That and all those letters she keeps writing.

I stopped writing to Joe a long time ago. After I told him I had TB, I didn't hear from him for quite a while. Finally he sent a V-mail:

Dear Marie-Claire,

I'm real sorry to hear about your TB, that's a tough break. I got that checkup like you asked me to and every- thing was clear. Don't worry the camp doctor told me you can't get it from kissing somebody just once. And speaking of kissing I have to tell you that I met somebody and she's real special—an English girl. Remember that farm family I told you about? Well Margaret is one of their daughters.

After that he went on and on for several boring lines about her before finally closing with, *Don't worry about me. I'll be fine. It's you who has got to take care. I'd still like to hear from you sometimes. All the best, Joe.*

So much for my letters keeping him going, and seeing my face at night just before he closes his eyes. Now that he's got Margaret to keep him company, he doesn't need me—the TB girl—ruining his party. I will never write to him again.

As for Signy, that photo of Sebastian—his handsome healthy face with its untrustworthy smile—is now taped to the wall beside her bed. She touches it every morning, when we are wheeled back to our rooms, as if for luck. At least he still writes to her occasionally, I'll give him that much, even if all it does is keep her hopes up. Even if he only seems to send one V-mail to every five or six of hers.

Still, it seems that some people have managed to have an actual romance. Just after cure hour the girl who occupied this bed before me, Louise Vogel, comes to our door. In the five months I've been here she has never been to visit Signy.

She flounces in looking healthy and lush, as if she's been living on thick cream. She hugs Signy like a long-lost friend. She barely acknowledges me as we're introduced and plunks down heavily on the bed, so that Signy is lifted right up into the air. Then she shoves her left hand practically under Signy's nose. The fourth finger sparkles with an engagement ring.

"Guess what! Morley's asked me to marry him!"

Signy draws a blank. "Who's Morley?"

Louise grows red. "Oh . . . that's right . . . I keep

thinking the whole world knows about me and Morley. But of course you wouldn't, you couldn't . . . know. Met him in December at this big Christmas banquet in the dining hall . . ."

She trails off, lowers long lashes.

"Look," she goes on, "I always meant to come back and see you. It's hard, you know to . . . see people. I mean, after you're getting better and they're . . ." She trails off again.

Signy smiles. "I understand. Really I do. I'm so happy for you. I think it's wonderful that you're getting married."

She doesn't mean it.

Louise bites at her lip. A couple of minutes in this room with us, the sick ones, and she's lost all her bounce.

"I'm also . . . I'm leaving. I just really, you know, wanted to come and say goodbye."

"You're leaving? You're being discharged?"

Louise nods. "My mum will be by to pick me up in about an hour."

Signy couldn't look any more shocked if Louise had just stood up and smacked her across the face.

Louise stays on and on and on.

Just when I think she's never going to leave, she finally trots out the door.

What an idiot, I think. Good riddance to her and her big ugly engagement ring.

Signy has already withered down under her covers.

It's a nice afternoon in late May. The windows are

open, a good-smelling breeze blows in. Before long, from across the sanatorium grounds, there's laughter and the sound of pots and pans being banged with spoons. The first time I heard this I didn't know what it was, not until Signy told me.

They're drumming Louise out—her roommates and fellow sufferers—saying their goodbyes.

Signy, on her back, stares at the spider pattern on our ceiling.

"I always thought it would be me who would leave here first," she says in a small voice. "I am glad for her, though. Really I am."

A little devil rears up inside me.

I say, imitating Louise's sappy tone, "Guess what? Morley's asked me to marry him!"

Shocked silence from Signy's bed.

My devil mouth continues, "The truth is she's a stupid ass to come in here and throw her good fortune in your face."

"Really?" She turns, startled.

"And you don't always have to act like such a saint to spare everybody's feelings. Always pretending to be so cheerful. Don't you ever get mad?"

She suddenly bursts into tears. I keep on, furiously— might as well, since I no longer believe that God will strike me down for the sin of anger. "I'm tired of it. It makes me grumpy. You're supposed to be grumpy in a place like this."

I fold my arms across my chest as she cries. I wait for a break in the sobbing.

Then I say, "Go ahead and hate me."

"I don't h-hate you."

Of course she doesn't. Signy's too nice. She would never hate anyone.

Exasperated, I look over at her and say, "Look, do you want me to cut your hair?"

It's the first thing I can think of.

"W-what?"

"Your hair, Signy. Should we cut it?"

"Really?" she says again, rubbing the tears from her eyes. "You'd really do that for me?"

She seems so grateful at the thought of this crumb of friendship that I blurt, "For sure, of course. I promise."

FOURTEEN

Not only does she want the haircut, but, my God, we have to look through every magazine she owns. After two days of looking, she finally shows me the picture of the hairdo she wants.

"That looks too complicated," I say.

She pouts.

I say, "Look, do you want me to cut your hair or don't you?"

"You don't have to if you don't want to," she answers in a hurt voice.

"I didn't say I didn't want to, Signy. Didn't I tell you that I would?"

She goes silent.

This whole thing is starting to drive me crazy.

"It's only hair. It'll grow back. Let's just get it done."

So now here we are. Me with a pair of scissors, and Signy sitting on the only chair in this big echoey bathroom. Her hair drips from her bath and her pajamas cling to her damp ribcage. I feel a pang of concern. Even for a TB patient Signy is pitifully thin, and—always, always, always—this reminds me of Luc.

The soap scum slurps behind us down the bath drain. As I begin to clip away her long pale hair, she starts to shiver.

"Are you cold?" I ask, alarmed.

"A little, but let's just keep going."

I grab a couple of towels from the rack, snuggling one over her knees and another around her shoulders. Except now she's shaking with chills.

"We'd better not do this," I say.

"Don't stop." She grabs for my hand as I let it fall away.

"This is a very bad idea, Signy. Let's not. I can't do this."

"Yes you can. Cut my hair. Cut it, like you promised."

She's so weak—what a stupid idea this was, yet here we are, and she's determined, and now I'm clipping as fast as I can, cutting my fingers in the process, blood everywhere. I keep going as my blood turns sections of her blond hair pink. I don't stop until all of it, curly like mine, is also short like mine.

Then I get us the hell out of the bathroom, back to our room, and into our beds.

Signy turns on her pillow. "That was fun!"

"Fun?"

"The most fun I've had in a very long time. Sometimes, Marie-Claire, you have to live dangerously, don't you think?"

Just the way she says it, like we're a couple of crooks on the lam, makes me laugh out loud. Then we're both laughing.

Dr. Yuen comes by on his rounds. He walks into the room in his usual jaunty manner, stops in his tracks, looks first at Signy, then at me.

"What have you two twins been up to?"

And, dear God, doesn't Signy shriek and get the giggles.

He shakes his head, puts his stethoscope to his ears, and smiles as he listens to her chest.

Nine o'clock the next morning, Mrs. Thompson arrives, pushing the scales, which are large and roll along on wheels. They clank through the door and lumber into our room.

Every TB patient dreads weigh day.

Even eating a huge breakfast will not trick these scales. We would have to put stones in our slippers to make any difference.

Signy doesn't want to go first. Neither do I.

Mrs. Thompson says, "For heaven's sake, somebody hurry up. Marie-Claire?"

So I'm first to step on the scales. They shake lightly beneath me as the balance bar, at chest level, flips up.

She adds the brass weights, quickly adjusts them. "There, see that, you silly girl? You've gained three pounds. Okay, Signy, you're next."

Signy clutches her dressing gown, fumbles around with tying the belt. Next she runs a trembling hand through her hair, steps on the scales.

Mrs. Thompson frowns and adjusts the brass weights. She removes some and puts on different ones. The balance bar comes to a halt and holds.

After a long pause she says, "You haven't lost any weight, Signy. In fact it seems you've gained some—just under half a pound."

After Mrs. Thompson leaves the room, Signy goes silent.

"Half a pound is half a pound," I tell her. "Better than nothing."

Still silence.

"Come on," I say. "This isn't a contest. Why don't you want to talk about it? You usually never want to *stop* talking."

"You want me to tell you the truth?"

"Sure."

Okay, now she's going to speak her mind—except maybe now I don't want to hear it. As Maman would say, careful what you wish for.

"I was twelve," she starts off, "when I was diagnosed with this stupid damn disease."

She's even swearing! What will pop out of her mouth next?

"Go on."

"I didn't even have, you know, breasts." She lowers her voice at the word "breasts."

"We're alone, Signy. And you got your breasts."

"Small ones," she says, with a sob.

"Oh, for Pete's sake, everybody's are different. Even cows."

"Yes, but now," she goes on, recovering herself, "when I try to stand up straight, I can't, because one shoulder is lower than the other, and my back is humped on one side. Even if I get out of this place, even if I dress up in the prettiest, most expensive clothes in the world, I won't look like a normal girl, and that's never going to change, now is it? Really, it won't."

What can I say to that? She's right. It won't.

"And who will love me?" she adds in a small voice.

From our balcony on the second floor of the west infirmary, we're up high enough to see the lake and hills through the treetops, yet below, the cut lawns are close enough for us to smell the grass.

At the end of cure hour, we see children out on the lawn for the first time. Playing catch in the sunshine with their nurse—four boys and five girls—and the tallest child among them is Josée!

Last time Maman was here, she told me, "Josée is doing so well! She's out of the infirmary and in the children's pavilion, and the doctors tell me she'll be home in no time! You wouldn't believe how much she's grown. I swear, she's tricking her TB bugs!"

This is the first time I've seen her since Christmas. It's a shock to see with my own eyes how in five months, without me, without her family, Josée has started to stretch up, as little girls do.

Papa, I haven't seen since the day Luc died.

I call out, "Josée!" and feel a pang in my heart.

She twists around. The ball drops from her hand. She comes running across the lawn. Then she stops below me, lifts her head. "Is that you, Marie-Claire?"

"Yes, yes!" I laugh, quickly wipe tears from my eyes. Blow her dozens of kisses.

She laughs, too, catching them like bubbles in her outstretched hands.

"*Je t'aime! Je t'aime!*" she cries.

Another little girl, as blond as Signy, runs up beside her.

"Hello!" she calls up. "Who are you?"

"This is my friend, Mary Elizabeth," says Josée, hugging her little friend close.

"Oh hello, Mary Elizabeth. I'm Josée's big sister."

The women on our balcony suddenly come alive in their beds. They begin to wave. Soon other women on the other balconies press against the screens. Everyone

112

is hungry for the sight of little boys and girls. Mothers longing to see their own children. Some, like me, missing their brothers and sisters. The girls and boys wave back, fluttering little hands from their little jackets. They play ring-around-the-rosie and chatter and shriek and laugh. Next, a clapping game led by their nurse.

We cheer and give them our biggest applause.

In my dreams I go to find Luc. I need to tell him how big Josée has grown. I fly back to our farm and have a bird's-eye view. I know that I won't find him down there, in the cramped house that smells of coal and sweat and dirty wash water and fatty homemade soap. And he won't be in the sun-filled, cow-smelling barn.

Only where the spring wind hits the face like a slap will I find him—across the field and over the woods to the rim of the valley.

In the tall grass I find a place to sink down and wait. The deep ravine below still flows with springwater—snow runoff from the fields—that then rushes through to the lake.

Suddenly I hear him—there! His feet swishing through the grasses. One hand tucked in his pocket. He hunkers down. Our shoulders touch.

To have him here again, right beside me!

I open my mouth to say something, but the words don't come.

He snatches at tufts of strawlike grass. There's a hole in the toe of one of his dusty black shoes. His socks are pulled up around his skinny ankles. They have a pattern of red hearts running up the sides. I have never seen these socks before.

Do the dead get brand-new things to wear? I stare at them as if they could tell me something about the world and about my brother that would make sense of this heartache.

In the morning Signy comes back from the bathroom, her hairbrush in her hand. She surprises me by stopping and sitting on the edge of my bed. She pulls blond tufts of hair out of her brush, rolls them into a little whirl, tucks the circle of hair into her pocket.

Today her dressing gown is a deep honey color. She owns seven beautiful dressing gowns, one for every day of the week.

Envy, another deadly sin I'm not supposed to be bothered about now that I've given up on God but that the Virgin Mary—in spite of my best efforts to cut Her out of my life, along with all the saints and so on—tells me I should pay attention to.

In my mind I tell the Blessed Mother to go away.

She just looks at me—resembling, as she does, Sister Thérèse—puts her hands in her lap, gets up from my mind. But I can still feel her, standing tall in a corner of the room in her cracked black shoes, watching me with arrowlike disapproval.

Signy, a flesh-and-blood girl, looks sadly into her hair-brush and confides, "He hasn't written back to me."

I turn and look at her.

Her lip trembles. A tear tumbles out of her eye and falls onto her hand, which is rosy in the morning light.

"Sebastian," she whispers.

She says his name like it's holy.

"Didn't he send you one last month?"

She shakes her head. "His last letter was seven weeks ago."

I think about this. Should I humor her? Or should I speak my mind—again?

Signy's a year older than me, yet at this moment she seems so much younger.

I think about Joe and his last letter to me, and how he went on and on about his English girlfriend.

"Why do you think he hasn't written, Signy? He's off doing God-knows-what with God-knows-who, while you're stuck here with TB. Don't you think it's time you stopped mooning over him and found somebody a little closer to home?"

Like one of those TB victims we see walking up the road every day. Some comfort that is, I say to the Blessed Mother, to the air.

But she's already left the room.

FIFTEEN

The blossoms of the crabapple tree just past the balcony screens are falling like snow onto the infirmary lawn. It's Sunday. The public address system is playing "Goodnight, Sweetheart" for the eleventh time since Tuesday.

Our beds are positioned in a long line near the screens.

I am reading a book of poetry, and Signy, in the bed in front of me, her short hair fluffed up over the pillows, is involved in her writing. Back in our room, Sebastian's photograph has disappeared, but for some reason Signy's gone from being in the dumps to being cheerful again— or at least to pretending that she is. She only writes one letter a week now, to her mother. She's taken up a new kind of writing, though, on the pages of a leather-bound diary with a tiny golden key, another gift from home. It's an activity that she goes at with a kind of ferocious energy.

As for me, I'm trying to get used to carrying on our strange friendship with the back of her head. Now that the warm weather has officially arrived, we stay out here on the balcony, along with our fellow sufferers. We don't walk back to our own rooms unless, on the way to the bathroom, we need to get something.

Mrs. McTigg, in the bed behind me, is constantly knitting, her needles clicking in frantic time to the gum she chews. We are only a week and a half into June and she's already made five pairs of socks this month for the soldiers overseas.

Mrs. Harder, in the bed behind Mrs. McTigg, cries because it's visiting day, and she already knows that nobody, again, will come to see her. Including her husband, who, it seems, has conveniently forgotten he has a wife. His name is Les.

I've privately nicknamed him Less Is Best.

Mrs. Harder doesn't share my sentiments. Whenever she isn't crying her eyes out, she calls him the Big Palooka.

Signy stops her writing long enough to pass me a note: *He's a low-life cad!*

I write back: *She married him!*

In the bed in front of Signy is a fourteen-year-old girl who is so sick from her TB that she hardly ever speaks. Whenever she does it's in a whisper, like she's afraid of what's going to happen next. The bed in front of the Whisperer held a newly married twenty-one-year-old woman named Helga Yakobvich, whose husband is serving overseas. Helga hemorrhaged from her lungs a couple of days ago during afternoon cure hour. There was so much blood that we all lay in shock as they hovered around her. They wheeled her to her room. She hasn't been back since.

When people move that close to the firing line, it's never a good sign.

Sure enough, yesterday morning Signy crept back from her bath, her big eyes bigger than normal.

"Helga's mother and father are here," she whispered to us. "The door to her room is closed. And the priest is here—I just saw him in the hallway."

Mrs. McTigg put down her knitting, blew her nose, and wiped her eyes.

"There now, poor thing," she said. "They'll bury her in her wedding dress."

In the space that was occupied by Helga is a new girl. She's around our age. I guess they think us young ones should be together. Her name is Julie Lafontaine, and last night as the stars were coming out she told us that her fiddle (which lies hidden in its black case on the chair beside her bed) is called Sweet Marguerite.

Julie said with a frown, "Why do they put me in the exact same spot where somebody died?"

"She didn't die there. She hemorrhaged there and died later in her room," Signy explained.

"What's the difference?" said Julie. "I don't want to be anywhere near dead people."

"Then you picked the wrong place," I told her. "People die here. They die like flies. You'd better get used to it."

"Oh, like you have?" she shot back. "Reading all the time? Hiding your nose in a book?"

This morning Julie filled her time fixing and unfixing her long black hair, filing her nails, applying lipstick while looking into a small hand mirror, and then rubbing it off again. She was trying to appear unconcerned. Yet her hands trembled.

This afternoon she's curled up like a child on the bed beside Mrs. McTigg, who is thrilled to have her there and is slowly teaching her how to knit.

"There you go, my dear . . . Yes, that's it . . . Loosen the wool up a bit . . ."

The nurses and nurse's aides and the orderlies come and go through all this. During cure hour, there is a no-talking rule that they usually enforce, more or less. Today, I guess they have better things to worry about. The fourteen-year-old—the Whisperer—has just been taken off the balcony. Well, we'll never see her again.

Julie's right, I do distract myself with books. What of it? There's nothing else to do. The good news is I can hold them up now without getting tired, and I can do this for hours and no one tells me not to. The bad news is there are so very many endless hours in which to do this, with nobody telling me not to.

I've decided I love the poet Walt Whitman, and his book called *Leaves of Grass*.

Today I have a little dictionary on the bed beside me. I've just looked up the words "diaphanous" and "libidinous." The first word I guessed right. The second I didn't. But I should have known it would be about sex, because Whitman thinks about sex a lot. He even thinks about sex when he looks at trees and streams.

Maybe that's what Tante Angeline was talking about when she told Maman reading would give me ideas. I don't think you'd find *Leaves of Grass* in our parish library.

Today, being Sunday, the chaplain makes his rounds. His shoes clatter against the gray balcony floors. He usually gives me only a passing smile. Today for some reason he stops at my bed.

I lift my eyes from the page. I give him my most grumpy look.

He glances at the wooden chair by the doorway.

"Do you mind?"

Seems he's going to stay anyway. So I nod.

Pulling the chair up to my bed, he sits. He looks first at his hands, then at me. He has dark hair and soft eyes. He's very young for a man of the cloth. Up close, he doesn't even have wrinkles around his eyes, and he smells good.

I wonder why the army hasn't claimed a young man such as him. Maybe he has flat feet. The army would reject him because of that. Or perhaps he once had TB.

Okay, so it's nice to have a young man—any young man—sit here, smelling as he does of aftershave and horses. And he's not a priest, so that means thoughts of sex are not off-limits.

Then he goes and spoils things.

"So, Marie-Claire. They tell me you don't want to see Father Boulanger anymore. Is it just him, or priests in general?"

I flatten my lips. Quite frankly, I wouldn't care if a priest came to me looking like Jesus Christ himself.

"You can tell me, you know," he says with a little smile. "I'm not a Catholic." And then, "I'm so sorry about your brother. And I knew your uncle Gérard. I visited him quite often. He was very fond of you. I'm . . . sorry for your losses."

My good mood, my barely held good mood, comes crashing down around me.

"My name is Frederick," he adds. "You can call me Fred if you like."

I wish now that he'd just go away.

He returns to looking at his hands, waits. What the hell does he want from me?

Mrs. McTigg's radio is playing the news. She's turned up the volume so we can all hear it over the music on the PA system. Today the news of the war is, as usual, not good.

I think about the post office back in St. Felix. About a day last summer when Luc looked at a posting on the door and saw that Frankie Boulet, the first of the twelve young men from our community who had gone to war, had recently been killed. Luc sat right down on the steps and I sat beside him. Just then we saw Frankie's little sister, Roxanne, come out of Drapeau's grocery with their mother and get into their truck and drive away.

121

"They'll have a nice funeral for him, right?" Luc said at last.

We watched the dust settle along the straight dirt road that led out of town. We watched until the truck was out of sight. Then Luc stood up. It was a hot day and little beads of sweat had collected around his hairline. I looked at him standing there, framed by the summer sky. I suddenly thought about him all grown up and taller than me—it could happen, that he'd get to be taller. But this picture stunned me. So when Luc finally said, "You didn't answer my question, Marie-Claire," all I could do was sit there like a damn fool thinking about him as a grown man, and what that would be like to look up at my brother instead of down.

Disgusted, he picked up his rifle and said, "Okay, ignore me then, like you usually do." And off he went to shoot gophers.

I look at Fred and say, "My brother's dead. Are you going to tell me that God loves me?"

Silence. Now maybe he'll leave since I've questioned the intentions of the Almighty.

Not a chance. Fred stays put, his backside practically glued to the chair, and I can tell he's thinking hard. His forehead, with that healthy smooth skin, suddenly crinkles up and his eyes turn slightly red.

Then, just when I think he might actually go, his body slumps slightly.

"Do you know any card tricks?" he asks with a sigh.

"Card tricks?"

"Here, let me show you."

He reaches into his pocket, fumbles around, pulls out a worn deck of cards, fans them face up on my blanket, and says seriously, "Come on, Marie-Claire. It's time you had some fun. Pick the queen of hearts. I'll make her disappear."

So I find her. His hands flutter like birds. He does make her disappear. But then he gets up and wanders off. He's gone for a long time.

Waiting for him, I nod off like a tired old lady.

I wake with a start, and there he is standing over me holding the queen of hearts in his hand.

I say, "You're a terrible magician."

"Made her reappear, didn't I?" He smiles.

After he goes away, I pick up *Leaves of Grass* and open it to the poem I'd been reading. A queen of hearts topples out from between the pages. I find another peeking out from under my pillow. A third is propped, half in flight, against the balcony screen.

From out on the infirmary lawn, now showered with apple blossom petals, a breeze comes dancing in. The third card flies from the balcony screen, lands on the hills of my knees, tumbles into my hands.

I pick up the card. I stare for a long time into the face of the queen. I wait for her lips to suddenly part, for words of hope to appear. And all at once I'm remembering Oncle Gérard's final words to me.

So you made it, my little queen of hearts. I knew you would.

SIXTEEN

X-ray, fluoroscopy, and more air to keep the pneumothorax going, to keep my right lung collapsed. In the conference room, Dr. Grant shoves my chest X-ray up against the light. The lesion, I can plainly see, is still there. I hate the sight of it.

"I thought it would have shrunk by now," I say, flattened with disappointment. "It's been like that for months."

Then, thinking the unthinkable, I say, "What if it grows?"

"It's not growing, Marie-Claire. In fact there's every indication that it may be shrinking slightly, that the pneumothorax is working. You have to be a patient patient."

He smiles a little at the joke he's just made.

"Will it ever go away?"

"That's what we're hoping," he says, putting a hand on my shoulder—something he did when he was delivering the bad news that it was growing.

I'm in a very foul mood when I get back to my bed on

the balcony. So much for being Oncle Gérard's little queen of hearts. Six months of TB, and I've had just about enough of this endless crap, and of being the "patient" patient.

We're lined up on the roof of the west infirmary, about twenty of us girls and women. We're all naked, taking the sun as part of our treatment, and we've been doing this once a day for a couple of weeks. At least it's a break in the routine.

I've been used to getting brown as a berry by working in the summer sun, but that was always just my arms and hands and face. Now every inch of me is brown from all this useless lying around. In fact everybody looks healthy even though we're all still as weak as sick cats.

With no nurses in sight up on the rooftop, the no-talking-during-cure-hour rule has been abandoned. Under the bright June sky, Mrs. McTigg, whose naked breasts sag around her like a couple of muskmelons, says, "I wonder what shenanigans they'll get up to this year."

This sets up a bit of chatter from all the ladies around us about something called the Annual Patients' Picnic.

I turn over onto my stomach and say to Signy, "We can't go. So what's all the excitement about?"

Signy pushes her pillow down, rests her chin on her hands. She lazily turns her head, her blue eyes flecked with green in the sunlight.

"They build a stage right down on the lawn by the trees. They set up a big tent behind it as a kind of changing room. They put on skits. Last year the doctors drove an old Model T right onto the lawn. And there's music and food and a baseball game and, when it gets dark, fireworks. We can see it all from our beds."

"Where do they get fireworks? There's a war going on."

"Oh, honestly, Marie-Claire," she says with a wheezy sigh, "you are such a wet blanket sometimes, really you are. They're doing this to cheer us up. Don't you want to be cheered up?"

No, I think to myself, I don't. Do they actually believe that some idiotic picnic's going to help with the general all-around misery here in the land of TB exiles?

But yet, sure enough, at the beginning of the third week of June, the "great day" arrives. By two o'clock in the afternoon people have started to gather down on the lawn. I'd like to ignore them, although it's impossible. They're cranked up at full volume, like a big flock of birds that won't shut up and won't fly away. I want to put a pillow over my head.

"No more resting today!" Signy tells me, her eyes flashing. "We'll be celebrating until eleven o'clock tonight, at least."

Dear God, they've planned a marathon.

People just keep arriving, streaming onto the lawn. Spreading their blankets on the grass, milling around in hats and summer pants and colorful dresses.

The rest of us, all of us jolly old TB derelicts, are

propped up against white pillows in our white beds all along the balconies of the east and west infirmaries.

The people below get to their feet for the national anthem. Who the hell are all these people? Ambulant patients, for sure, and in the crowd of heads I recognize some off-duty staff, but as for the rest of them . . . ?

After that, as people sit again, Dr. Grant, onstage at the microphone, welcomes everybody, his voice loud and echoing over the PA system. He's chosen a yellow necktie that is, I guess, supposed to be festive. But, honestly, it's so big he could use it to hang himself.

Next comes the sanatorium orchestra. Ambulant patients, mostly older men—a drummer, a bassist, a fiddler, and an accordionist—drag themselves onto the stage. There are some other more lively ones, boys of around our age, one at the piano, another with a guitar, and a third one with a trumpet, who is tall, with dark-blond curly hair. I have to say that the trumpet guy stands out from the rest in his brown pants and brown vest with a gleaming white shirt, open at the neck.

He lowers his trumpet and puts his lips to the microphone and then something starts to happen to me. He sings "Tangerine," a new song that's been playing lately on the radio, and certain parts of my anatomy that were asleep—parts I'd almost forgotten about—come fully awake and tingling. Then he steps back, lifts his trumpet, and begins to play the song again, meltingly sweet way down there on that stage.

Now I'm aware of something else, and it's heart stopping—like he's defying his TB. At the foot of the stage, where others have noticed it, too, a couple of people with cameras start snapping pictures.

"That's Jack Hawkings—the guy with the trumpet," Signy says, quietly turning around in her bed, pushing her pillow down so I can see her better. "He's a legend."

"You know him?"

"Like I said, a legend. Three years ago, at sixteen, he was the youngest boy ever to play with the Murray Kaye Band, and he got to play with them not just around Winnipeg but touring all over the country. Mum used to send me newspaper clippings about them. Then about a year ago, Jack broke down with TB. I heard that he ended up here at Pembina Hills, but this is the first time I've actually seen him in person. Guess he's getting better."

Suddenly I remember. Back in December, those notes from Luc that he asked someone else to write for him. The day I visited Luc, the day he was dying, and the tall boy who got out of bed to tell me how sorry he was. It was Jack—Jack Hawkings.

So how did he get from leaning like a scarecrow against the door of my brother's room to standing up there on that stage? Still sick, I'm thinking, but also very much alive.

The song ends, Signy turns around again, and the band starts right into "Red River Jig."

Julie Lafontaine presses against the balcony screens. She's watching it all, her face fierce with longing.

Mrs. McTigg, knitting again, calls out, "So if you can't be down there with them, get out your fiddle and play anyway."

Julie's fiddle sits like a bump on a log on the chair beside her bed. The ward girls aren't permitted to touch it—not even to wipe dust or stray raindrops from the case.

"I know this one," she says in a real soft voice. "My grandpa taught it to me."

Suddenly, she reaches over and pulls the fiddle case onto her bed. She opens it, lifts out her instrument, which is not at all pretty the way I imagined a fiddle named Sweet Marguerite would be.

We watch as she fools around trying to get it tuned. Now all we want is for her to hurry up before the song has ended.

At last, she stands up on her bed, tucks the fiddle under her chin, poises the bow across the strings, says, "Well, here goes nothing, ladies . . ." and starts to play.

Below, people look up to see where this other sound is coming from. Soon half the audience has turned to see her. This girl in blue pajamas, black hair sticking to the sweat on her face—playing her heart out, that's for sure. Not in tune and not in time, either, but that doesn't seem to slow her up any.

The boys in the band finally notice her and laugh and shout to each other. She keeps playing, and my God, if she isn't also flirting with them. The whole band lurches into another round of "Red River Jig." It descends into quite a mess, but the crowd loves it anyway. The musicians quit playing one by one, until Julie's the only one still at it. The audience below turns to her, hands raised in applause, whistling and cheering.

At last she falls laughing onto her bed, Sweet Marguerite lying across her chest. Yet no sooner does she do that than she's struggling up again to wave at everybody.

The boys wave at her. Then they notice the rest of us waving back at them, too.

Later, sandwiches and cake and watermelon and ice cream are served out on the lawn and on the balconies. I'm actually enjoying myself. Maybe a picnic wasn't such a stupid idea after all.

A sharp whistle comes from below. I drop my sandwich and press my hands, my face, against the screen and look down.

The Legend—looking straight up at me! He's thin in his loose-fitting vest and white shirt and dark brown pants, but he seems lit up somehow.

"Hi," he says with a smile that lights him up even more.

"Hello," I say, smiling back, heart pounding—and not from TB palpitations.

"Hello," he says again. "I'm Jack, Jack Hawkings."

"Marie-Claire—Côté. Luc's . . . sister."

"I knew it was you!" he says, his smile widening. "So, you're enjoying it all?"

"Oh yes, very much. Very, very much," I babble.

"Good. Oh good. That's good. I'm glad. Did you have lunch?"

"Oh yes, I'm having lunch. It's very, very good."

You stupid girl, think of something else to say to him.

Too late—with a small hesitant wave of his hand, he turns as if to go.

"I liked your music," I say quickly. "'Tangerine' was very nice."

"Oh, I'm so glad," he says, turning to me again.

I press on. Words just fall out of my mouth. "In fact I loved it. I loved it all. You should . . . you should just keep playing and never give up."

I don't know what the hell's made me say that, about playing and never giving up.

He suddenly blushes. "Well, actually, it's the first time I've played for an audience in a real long time."

Now I'm blushing, too.

I feel a small thump on my bed. It's Signy easing up beside me.

"Hello, Jack Hawkings," she says shyly. "How's Winnipeg?"

"Winnipeg? You're from Winnipeg?"

"Yes."

"What a small world!"

"Yes," she repeats, and at this she leans up against me, and I can feel her trembling. Well, maybe we're both trembling.

Julie suddenly joins us on the bed.

Jack points his finger at her. "You're the fiddler!"

"That's me!" she says proudly. "Where's your friend?"

"Which one?"

Julie, in a pouting, flirty way, says, "Go and get them both, and tell them they'd better not keep us ladies waiting."

"I'm on my way," Jack says, with a look in my direction. He disappears into the crowd.

Suddenly, Signy sinks back against the pillows and goes quiet. She's wearing a cream-colored satin bed jacket. She got all prettied up for the picnic.

I turn to her, raise an eyebrow. "What's the matter?"

"I just . . . I realized something."

"You might as well say it. Since I know you're going to anyway."

She gives me a look. Shakes her head. Stays on the bed with me. I feel a thread like some spidery thing connecting us.

I nudge my shoulder against hers.

At last, she says softly, "I wonder if I'm ever going to leave this place."

"Are you crazy?" Julie pipes up. "Of course you're going to leave this place. We all are. Personally, I can't wait."

"Julie's right," I say. "Let's just enjoy this day, okay?"

"Yes, let's," Signy says, her smile returning.

Simple as that then, we do.

Julie sits cross-legged at the end of the bed and starts

up another jig. Signy and I lie back while she entertains us, and the late afternoon sun warms our skin.

Jack comes back with his buddies. Julie keeps on fiddling. He puts his hands on his hips and grins up at us, while the piano player and the guitar player begin to clap and laugh. They show off, linking arms, wheeling out, bumping into people who are sitting on blankets, people walking around with plates of food, causing pointed stares and angry complaints.

When Julie can't play anymore, she stops and puts down her fiddle. I throw her a pillow. With one hand she catches it, flips it behind her head. She leans back, and then quickly sits up again to look down at the boys, who have stopped dancing.

Jack introduces his friends. The guitarist is Robert Fleury, and I think from the look of him that he is Métis, like Julie.

The piano player, Sandy McLeod, has thick auburn hair. He stares for a long time at Signy, then gives her a slow cheeky wink that makes her blush darkly from her neck up.

I link my arm through hers at her sudden shyness about all these happy boys under our balcony.

Julie, not at all shy, flirts with Robert. "Next time I play my fiddle for you, it'll be down there on the grass."

"It'll be sooner than that. I'm coming up there to visit you."

"When? I won't wait forever, Romeo."

SEVENTEEN

RULES CONCERNING VISITS BETWEEN AMBULANT AND INFIRMARY PATIENTS

Patients in outside buildings may visit infirmary patients *of the same sex*, with a pass, on Tuesdays and Saturdays before or after rest hours. Male and female patients may also visit each other during those times, with a pass, *in the infirmary common room only*.

The moon is almost full and so bright it's hard to sleep. A strong breeze snaps the screens. The night air is warm and alive. I'm restless as hell.

Julie sneaks out of bed at midnight, when everybody but me is asleep. My eyes are open wide. She comes to my bed, and I stare up at her, standing with the moonlight on her shoulders, nervously combing her hair with her fingers.

"I'm meeting Robert on the fire escape. He's bringing a surprise," she whispers. "If you're not out of that bed soon, I'm going without you, and you'll disappoint your surprise."

Disappoint? My heart begins to thud.

She whips back my covers. I feel small and exposed. She walks away, not waiting for me another second.

The nurses are always on the lookout. If you spend too long in the bathroom, especially at night, they come looking to see if you've gotten yourself into trouble.

I could pretend I'm on my way to the bathroom.

I wish my hair, at least, were clean.

I wish my dressing gown weren't so ugly.

I leave the sleeping balcony and pass into the hallway. Julie's already disappeared and there's nobody else in sight. It's quiet except for the raspy breathing coming from the rooms where the sickest ones lie, waiting for the hand of God to come and sweep them off the face of the earth.

I'm dizzy with the fear of being caught. My one lung, the one that's supposed to be doing all the work, seems to be struggling more than usual.

I count my steps. Step eighty-four and I've almost reached the end of the hall. Step ninety-one and my hand's on the fire-escape door. I push, then lean against it with all my weight.

It opens suddenly. I burst out onto the wrought-iron fire escape.

The trees and the sky and the moon and the night wind all make me catch my breath.

Then I see, leaning against the railing, the Legend himself, Jack Hawkings!

I trip and lose my balance. He quickly catches me. I notice that his arms are trembling.

"Sorry!" I say.

Sorry is the first word out of my mouth!

"Not about being here, I hope," he says with a nervous laugh, letting me go.

"I'm not! Look at this night! Look at you!" I'm babbling now. "Where are Julie and Robert?"

"Gone somewhere. I brought you a present, Marie-Claire. Made it for you in occupational therapy. We make boring stuff there, like hand-tooled wallets that nobody wants. But I did want to make something different for you. Hope you like it."

The excitement of just being here with him out in the open night is almost too much for me.

He takes my shoulders and sits me on one of the steps.

"Wait here," he instructs. "This'll only take a minute."

"Where are you going?"

"It's a surprise. Be patient."

I laugh. "That's all I ever do!"

The stairs shake as he walks down. Then silence. I don't hear him at all.

"Where did you go?" I say.

"I'm here!" he whispers hoarsely. "Out on the road."

Starting somewhere up around the ambulant patient cottages, a hilly service road runs down behind the infirmaries.

The moon has turned everything pale. Below me, the wind in his hair, his unzipped jacket billowing, Jack starts to run down the service road. Something behind him drags and bounces and lifts. Tosses and tumbles in the air. He turns, feet crunching on the gravel, running backward.

A kite! It climbs higher. The moon makes a path down the sky, lighting its face and a long tail of ribbons.

"What do you think?" he says, giving his attention to its flight.

"It's the prettiest thing I've ever seen!"

"You have to feel it tug in the wind, Marie-Claire—to get the full effect."

I pick my way down the clanking metal stairs until my feet find the ground. I have not been out of bed for this long since Christmas. I worry that my legs will give out, but they don't. I reach him and he pulls me back against him, inside the circle of his arms. The smell of his sweat and aftershave and the nearness of him are distracting.

The kite rises against the wind. I place my hand on his hand, the one holding the string, feel the softness of his skin, the fine hairs along his slender fingers, and the electric pull of the kite, alive like a bird high above us.

The wind suddenly dies. Just like that. The kite dives toward the treetops and lands in a tangle of branches.

A car comes down the road, headlights shining. We sink together into the darkness under the fire escape. Jack's arms come around me again as the white lights flash past and the car rolls away toward town.

"That was close." His breath travels all hot sparks against my neck, my cheek, and my ear.

"I have to go now," I say, my heart beating far too fast for all kinds of reasons. "Thank you for my surprise. I . . . loved it."

"Just newspaper and glue and balsa wood," he says as I slip out of his arms. "Not meant to last. Can't you stay a little longer?"

I'm stumbling up the stairs, panting now, my good lung about to burst.

"Marie-Claire!"

I stumble again, turning to him.

"I wanted to tell you on the day of the picnic. I liked your brother, Luc. He was a good kid."

I grip the iron railing as he continues. "For a while there, when he first bunked in with us, he talked about you a lot—well, the whole family, but you especially. I figured you must be pretty special. I just never pictured in my mind when I was writing those notes for him—"

"Were you there when it happened?"

Maybe I've shocked him, coming out so bluntly like that with such a question.

Instead he seems relieved. "We were all there. Robert and Sandy and me."

My legs are finally no longer able to hold me up. I sink down on the stairs.

His footsteps shake the iron steps as he moves swiftly up and eases down to sit beside me.

We're quiet for a time.

"He was a funny kid," Jack begins. "Sick as he was, he told us the wildest stories. Did you ever hear the one about the Shadow Man?"

Suddenly I'm on the hill overlooking the ravine back home, sitting there with Gérard and Luc and Josée, making bird calls, waiting for the imaginary Shadow Man to appear.

Oncle Gérard lowering his voice and saying to our little sister, *He's half human and half ghost, Josée. He can be anywhere, anytime. He can even change shape when he wants to fly.*

And then all at once that hawk circling far above us, making its eerie cry.

Ohhh! says Josée. How does he do that?

It's magic, says Luc.

"He was crazy about flying," Jack is saying. "He'd tell about how the Shadow Man could turn into a hawk. We could almost see it happening."

Maybe if Luc had lived, he would have become a storyteller, like Oncle Gérard.

But he didn't live, and in all my life, if I get to live a long time, I will never get over the unfairness of it.

"That night, when he died, we were there like I said, and at some point he started to cough. It just went on and on, and finally he coughed up a lot of blood, more than I've actually ever seen come out of one human being. He . . . I guess what happened was he hemorrhaged."

"He was so small," I say, my heart breaking.

Jack sits very still. He stops talking for a while. The night wind sighs in the trees.

At last he goes on. "His nurse came around and sponged him down, tried to make him comfortable, even though he was really not of this world anymore. We'd already asked if we could sit up with him, stay with him all night instead of being taken out onto the balcony. Because we all knew . . . everybody knew . . .

"So there we were, just kind of waiting for it to happen. But I'd been real impressed by how you came by in your wheelchair that afternoon. You know, sat beside him like you did. Told him all that stuff about your lives together, just like he could hear you. So all I did, honest to God, Marie-Claire, was just continue with it. My brother's in the air force. So I told Luc about Ted being a flyer. I thought if he could hear me at all, it might make him think about some kind of a good future. It wasn't long after that he died. In the end it was quite peaceful. It was still a shock to us, though, him finally going so quickly . . ."

I stagger to my feet and grip the rail again, feeling like an old woman. Jack gets up, too. We face each other.

At last I say the only thing I can think of. "I'm glad you were there."

He takes my hand, looks at it, and turns it over in his own. He quickly lifts it to his lips and kisses my palm, leaving an electric imprint. I watch him walk down the stairs, then back up the service road toward the ambulant patient cottages.

When the shadows finally enfold him, I bring my hand, just where he kissed it, to my face. I hold it there for a while and look out at the place where he vanished. I glance again at the moon, then finally go inside.

I pass down the quiet hallway and back to the balcony, where I go and stand by Signy's bed. She's awake, looking up at me like a wraith in the moonlight, and for a moment it makes me shiver. It's as if Luc has just slipped between us and placed his cold hands on our cheeks.

"Hi," I say, pushing this image aside. "I just saw Jack."

"Jack? You mean on the fire escape?"

"Yes."

"Was—Sandy there, too?"

"Sandy? No."

"I just thought . . ." she trails off. "So, did you have a good time?"

"Yes."

"You look cold."

"I guess I am. A bit."

"I hope you had fun."

"He made me a kite."

"Ohhh," she breathes, "how beautiful! Did you get to fly it?"

"Yes."

And I felt his arms so warm and alive around me, and his kiss, like a hot spark, on my palm. I don't tell her this. But I figure, at the very least, I can tell her how it felt to fly a kite, such a beautiful kite, under the moon.

Queen of Hearts

Summer 1942

EIGHTEEN

August 18, 1942. In total, I lost twenty pounds, but in the past eight months, since I've been here at Pembina Hills San, I've gained back twelve. I'm stronger, too. They let me walk now, up and down the halls, fifteen minutes every day. However, as I make my way on my own two legs to the conference room, I'm nervous. I've been summoned there, and I don't know why.

X-ray, lab, a few more steps, a sharp left turn. There they are, waiting for me, as I enter the room.

"Sit, Marie-Claire," Dr. Yuen says with a neutral smile.

The lights are very bright. I slide into the chair and smile back, just a little. I fold my arms, not quite knowing what to do with them, so that one reaches around my waist, while the other arm covers my chest, my heart, like a protection.

Dr. Grant leans forward.

"Your sputum counts came back negative today. You're no longer infectious," he says. "Also your friend, as well—"

"Signy?"

Dr. Grant sits back, takes off his glasses, and tosses them on the table beside him.

"No. But you are ambulant, Marie-Claire, you and the Lafontaine girl—Julie. You both still have TB, of course—that hasn't changed—however we feel you're well enough to be discharged from the infirmary. We're putting you both in Creighton Cottage. Just above the main building. It's the next step to working up your strength and getting you better."

"But not Signy?"

Yuen and Grant look at each other.

"No, not Signy. Not just yet, although we're hopeful . . ." Dr. Grant trails off, nodding his head.

I walk out of the conference room and down the hall. Have they told her yet? Does she know?

She's sitting on the edge of her bed on the balcony when I get back, looking down at her slippers. When she looks up and sees me and gives me a big brave smile, I know that she knows.

I sit on the bed beside her.

She's still smiling bravely as she reaches over and pulls my hand from my lap into her own, gripping it tightly. "Julie just told me . . ."

"Yes," I say, a lump gathering in my throat.

I don't want to feel what I'm feeling. I don't want to be swallowed up by her sadness and her terrible loneliness and her need to be best friends with me.

I watch the smile slide off her face as she keeps gripping my hand.

At last she whispers brokenly, "Five years of this . . . of saying goodbye to people."

"I'll still be here. I'll be at Creighton Cottage. It's not far—"

She pulls away and looks at me. "It's hard for people to visit . . . I know that . . ."

"It'll be like . . ." I struggle desperately to find something to say. "Listen, it's like this. When I'm looking at the full moon, maybe you'll be looking at it, too, at the exact same time. I'll send a thought out to you. And you'll send a thought out to me."

"You mean, not like TB friends? Like . . . like kindred spirits?"

Dear God, no, I think, not like kindred spirits. Keeping my voice as light as possible, I say, "Sure."

After lunch, on my way to the bathroom, I meet Mrs. Thompson in the hall as she's coming out of one of the rooms. I've never had an actual conversation with her. She never seems to know what to say to me, or to any of the younger patients, for that matter. Although when she's taken a shift on night duty, she sometimes sits with the older patients and listens while they talk. Lately, it's been with Mrs. McTigg, whose children, like all visiting children, aren't allowed on the infirmary wards.

On Sundays Mr. McTigg—Donald—brings them from

High Bluff, where they live, and the whole family, including Donald, stands out on the lawn and waves to her and she talks to them through the balcony screens.

After they leave, Mrs. McTigg cries. She's been in the infirmary for three years. When I overhear Mrs. Thompson and her talking—their voices hushed in the night—it's always the same sad refrain. How hard it is to watch your children grow up as they stand on some lawn, and you're never allowed close enough to hold them, and you hardly know them anymore.

Mrs. Thompson falls in beside me. "I hear you're leaving us. I'm pleased for you."

"Thanks."

"You seem a little pensive, Marie-Claire. Let's go down to my office."

I'm surprised by this invitation. I follow her down the hall.

Red Lips, who is also on days this week, looks up from the desk in the tiny nurse's office. She and Mrs. Thompson must share some kind of invisible nurse's Morse code because she gets up and leaves, shutting the door behind her.

A small couch rests against one wall, brown with cracked leather. Mrs. Thompson indicates that's where I should sit. I expect that she'll go and sit behind the desk. Instead, she sits with me on the couch.

The wind outside the window breaks in little rattling gusts.

I'm crowded by fears. Will there be nurses at Creighton Cottage to take care of us? Will Dr. Yuen still be my doctor?

Mrs. Thompson says, "You're a very bright girl, Marie-Claire."

"Oh," I say, twisting my fingers together at this compliment, wondering where it will lead.

"Sometimes," she says, "some people are, for lack of a better word, quite sympathetic to their surroundings, and of course are sensitive to other people. As you seem to be."

I have no idea what she's talking about. I raise my eyes and look into hers as she goes on, "It can be troublesome, at times, to turn off the heart's concerns."

Okay, maybe she's talking about herself. All those heart-to-heart midnight conversations with Mrs. McTigg.

She continues, "When you've been at Creighton Cottage for a while—when you're stronger—you'll be given a work-up program to build your strength. Maybe you'd like to come back here and work for me."

"Oh . . . I don't know . . ."

"As a ward girl—but only if you want to," she adds quickly. "Of course, in a few days our teacher, Miss Neustadt, will visit you and Julie, get you girls back to your studies. I'm sure you'll appreciate that."

So much is coming at me all at once.

"Is there something on your mind, Marie-Claire?"

I hesitate.

"Yes, I guess. Signy."

"Ah, good. I'm glad you've brought this up." Mrs. Thompson seems relieved. "There's been a marked improvement in her cure since, well, since December. When you came to us."

She looks at me meaningfully. "Surely you knew that."

"What do you mean *improved*?"

"Her cure's been difficult and continues to be difficult. She tries to put a cheerful face on things. She's always done that. It's her way of coping. However, some of our patients have been here in the infirmary for ten, twenty years. All she has to do is look around. I worry about how she'll be when you leave. She doesn't seem to need to pretend with you. That's the difference between you and, well, the others. It seems that with you she's had more . . . hope."

"Hope?"

"Yes."

"But I'm not going anywhere! I'm just going to Creighton Cottage! And I'll . . . I'll come back to see her."

"Good, that's good," says Mrs. Thompson. "She's very much alone. Her parents are nice enough. Her mother sends her things. However they rarely visit and so I really hope that you will."

I think about Signy on that first day and what she said to me: *I think it's fate that I found you and you found me. I just know we're going to be wonderful friends!*

Mrs. Thompson stands. Apparently our visit is over.

"There's a lot of fear in the general public about TB, as I'm sure you know," she says as I, too, get up off the couch. "That's why you hardly see any visitors and why patients just try to make some kind of life for themselves. Once you and Julie have moved over to Creighton Cottage, you'll see even more of that." She pauses. "Which reminds me—on my lunch break I ran into a young man, Jack Hawkings." She looks at me sharply. "Surely you remember him? The trumpet player?"

I feel my cheeks flush hotly.

"He asked about you and wanted me to give you this." She takes a folded piece of paper from the pocket of her crisp uniform, handing it to me. I slip it away in my dressing gown.

She offers her hand, which I take.

"Good luck to you, Marie-Claire. You'll be missed. Especially by Signy."

I am sent on my way.

I'm almost back to the balcony when I meet Dr. Yuen coming up the hall. His hair is wet, as if he has just gotten caught in the rain. Except the sun has been shining all day.

He smiles when he sees me looking at his hair, runs a hand over it.

"I got dunked in Pembina Lake. Took a couple of hours off and went out in the sailboat. Which capsized. Got dunked," he repeats.

When I don't smile, he puts a hand on my back and steers me onto the balcony.

"I've got news for you, by the way. Your little sister, Josée, is leaving us. Going home."

"Home?" I turn to him.

Maman's visits have become less and less frequent, with one excuse after another. First it was because of the war rationing on gasoline. Next it was because she caught a cold and didn't want to infect us. After that, well, she still had the same excuse—"a cold."

Last month I didn't see her at all. Only a letter saying, *Don't forget to say your rosary, even if you refuse to see Father Boulanger. His feelings are hurt, Marie-Claire, he's a human being just like the rest of us. And it's heavy on the poor man's heart (he keeps mentioning it to me) that the last time he saw you he was so concerned about Luc that he didn't ask for your confession.*

"Marie-Claire," Dr. Yuen says, "I'll arrange for you to have a visit with Josée before she's discharged. And by the way, I'm still your doctor. I'll be keeping close tabs on you, young lady."

He turns and goes whistling down the hall, like a happy man with a completed mission.

I go out to the balcony and fall flat on my back on my bed. My head fills up with a memory.

A windy August day with bright sunshine, just like this one, and a picnic by the lake.

I'm a helpful girl of nine. As I pull things out of the picnic basket, Luc runs screaming and laughing into the big waves.

"Come and play with me, Marie-Claire . . . !"

The car's parked along the shore. Doors and windows open to the wind. Maman sitting on a blanket, Josée in her arms. Papa, a cigar hanging festively from his mouth, pulls off his shoes and socks, rolls up fluttering pant legs for the sun to beat down on his fish-white skin.

"Go and be with your brother," he urges. "He needs you."

I hurry and change into my bathing suit behind some trees. I run to join Luc in the warm waves. He's slippery, fighting me until I drop him. He disappears and, seconds later, comes back up, gasping for air, laughing, flinging himself at my neck, pulling us both under.

We bob up again. Papa's on the shore, head thrown back, laughing, his face framed by the summer sky.

Just a moment, like any other family moment, that sticks out in my mind because it was a shiny day and we were happy.

If Papa had been given a choice over which of his children would live, would he have chosen me?

I sit up, breathe in the summer wind, and pull Jack's note from my pocket.

> *Prince Albert Cottage*
> *(a stone's throw away from Creighton Cottage!)*
> *Dear Marie-Claire—I understand, through the sanatorium grapevine, that you are well enough to leave the infirmary at last. Hallelujah! Yours, Jack Hawkings*

NINETEEN

Next morning, after breakfast, Julie and I are told to get dressed in regular clothing. While we're getting ready, Signy, the only one of us who ever makes long-distance calls, as they are so expensive, asks Nurse Thompson, "May I make a phone call to Winnipeg?"

"Of course, and take all the time you need," Mrs. Thompson tells her, with a quick look at me.

I look away and fiddle with the fastenings of a small suitcase of clothing, one that Maman brought me from home some time ago. I open the lid, with its tired dark leather, and look inside. I take out the cream-colored faille dress I wore the night I met Joe. I put it on and discover that even with this weight gain it hangs on me. I pull the sash tightly around my waist, knot it, and get on with packing. I open the drawer in my bedside table. There's very little, really, to show that I've been here since last December: a comb, a brush, pencil, notepad, and the *Welcome to Pembina Hills Sanatorium* booklet. The pressed notes from

Luc. Even if they aren't in his handwriting, they are at least his own words, words that are precious to me.

There is, as well, the photo of Father Boulanger's dog, Cadeau, and it seems I should take that, too. I also find the three cards—the queens of hearts—that Fred the chaplain conjured up that Sunday he stopped by my bed to visit. Oh yes, and the rosary from Sister Thérèse that has been busily collecting dust ever since December.

Then, far back in the drawer, my fingers come into contact with a small box. I ease it out and flip up the lid.

The pearl ring, my birthday present from Signy.

She comes back from her phone call just as I'm snapping the box shut again.

"Oh," she says, looking at it in my hand.

She goes to her bed, pretends that the sheets need straightening, then suddenly sits, burying her face in her hands.

I go and sit on her bed and think about what I should do. I could put an arm around her. But I can't quite manage it. Instead, I sit and wait, wait as she cries for quite a while, big shuddering sobs. Finally she stops crying. With a broken sigh, she reaches for a tissue box, which falls to the floor. I lean over to pick it up, get dizzy all at once, sit up and see stars, feel like fainting, take a couple of deep breaths, grab a handful of tissues, and hand them to her.

"Thanks," she says, sadly blowing her nose. "You okay?"

All I want to do is get out of here.

Twenty minutes later, Julie and I are at last outside in

the sun, pushed along in wheelchairs by two orderlies up the service road.

At Creighton Cottage, a nurse long past retirement age greets us.

"I'm Annie," she says with a tired smile. "Too old to be a miss and no longer anybody's missus. Just Annie, if you please. You'll be out on the balcony with three other ladies until October. Rules are the same. Bed rest—that is, until you start having meals up."

The view from our first-floor sleeping porch is of clumps of evergreen and the narrow road below. Right across the road is Prince Albert Cottage, where Jack stays. A little flame jumps up inside me. Annie shoves her arm in front of my face and points beyond where I'm looking to a gabled red-roofed building. In a flash, I call up the day of the train and Luc and me reaching that place, escaping from the winter wind.

"Main building," Annie offers. "It houses the business office, telephone office, meat and milk and grocery room, sewing room, main kitchen, dining hall, assembly hall, two floors of staff bedrooms and small apartments. Takes an army to run this place."

She leads us inside, down a hallway, past a bathroom, to our bedroom, as her prattle continues.

"We just admitted a merchant marine to the east infirmary, TB in both lungs, spent ten days eating hardtack on a lifeboat in the North Atlantic after the supply ship he was on got torpedoed—and there'll be plenty more just like him to keep us busy. Now get undressed, ladies, and don't worry about unpacking. Just slide those cases into that cupboard there."

She leaves. We get into our pajamas. Julie disappears down the hall to the bathroom. I go to our bedroom window. Below, at a clothesline, are two girls. One is dressed in regular clothes, the other in satin pajamas—and both are curvy and healthy looking. They talk and laugh like good friends while they hang out their wash.

Julie and I share our balcony with three older women. Helen and Tina, a couple of retired unmarried school-teachers, are off to themselves at the far end.

"They tell me they'll be renting a flat together in Winnipeg after they get their discharge. I wouldn't hold my breath that that's anytime soon," the third one, Rose, informs us.

She lowers her voice. "That big one, Tina? She left the San for a while, but her health broke down again, and, lickety-split, she's back here. Within six months! Wouldn't think from all the weight she's put on that there's a thing wrong with her. Got a cavity in her left lung, though, and that's bad, seeing as how they removed the right one the first time she was at the San. Ten years in total of chasing the cure—a life sentence, that is. Of course, she drinks like a fish, and Helen's no better. They deserve each other, if you ask me. Not that I'm unsympathetic. I'm just a realist. I says what I sees."

Rose is healthy-looking herself and fleshed out like some of the other ambulant patients I'm just starting to see. She's in her mid-forties or so and doesn't have a wedding ring.

"I can't tell you how happy I am to see you girls. It's been a dull deal around here, let me tell you, with those two for company." She goes on, "I'm one of the Hello Girls, you know—telephone operator at the main building, two hours a day, part of my work-up program, but you have to have the personality for it."

She also sorts incoming mail and sells stamps and toiletry items, like hair combs, toothpaste, Evening in Paris perfume, aftershave. However, what it seems she mainly does is wear the headphones and listen in on incoming and outgoing telephone calls.

We quickly find out that she can tell you:

1. Who is slated tomorrow morning for surgery.

2. Whose boyfriend or son or brother or husband has just died or gone missing in action overseas.

3. Who (with or without the bonds of holy matrimony) is going to have a baby.

4. Who is bootlegging beer, and for whom, for the not-so-secret bonfires and drinking parties that she claims are held regularly on the hill above Creighton Cottage.

5. Who shimmied out the bathroom window at midnight to join the boys on the top of that hill.

6. And who forgot her panties up there, to be discovered later by the night watchman, and which he then

retrieved and left on the clothesline for all to see—like a flag of sin—the following morning.

At noon Rose and the other two go for lunch in the dining room in the main building. A big quiet settles over Julie and me. Neither of us knows what to say now that we're alone.

Five years of this . . . of saying goodbye to people.

The lunch trolley breaks up the quiet, clanking onto the balcony, and I open my eyes to see Julie's Romeo, Robert Fleury.

"Here's your lunch, girls," he says with a huge smile.

Julie gives him a sly one back, then shrugs her shoulders at me.

"Work-up program, forgot to tell you."

"Two hours every day of pushing trolleys, and it isn't so bad," he says. "Lucky me, I get to sling trays. You should see what Jack Hawkings gets to do every afternoon at the east infirmary. Bedpans, don't ask. And Sandy, that lucky stiff, he just got his discharge. So he's free and clear."

He gives me my tray and saves Julie's for last. He bends close to her ear as she sinks down in bed, one arm flung around his neck.

I hear him whisper, "How about you, beautiful? Are you hungry?"

She whispers something back that I can't hear. Pretty soon they're both giggling.

I look away. I pick up my fork and start to eat.

Robert finally leaves, and when I dare to look over at her, Julie raises herself up, being careful not to upset the lunch he has arranged. The noontime sunlight spills over the bottom of her bed, her toes making little bumps under the covers. She contentedly begins to spoon mouthfuls of cream of celery soup into her pretty mouth.

I like this girl. She isn't desperate—she's easy to be with.

Then she says, "You're missing Signy, aren't you?"

Signy.

"Oh well," I say, "I can . . . I can always visit."

She looks into her soup. "But you will miss her. You seem like such good friends."

"What I am," I say, "is just so glad to be free of that place."

"Oh for sure." Julie puts down her spoon. "And . . . and I'm glad we've got each other, aren't you?"

"I am, I sure am," I tell her as she smiles at me.

TWENTY

Next day I'm waiting to see my sister. The orderly's left me in a wheelchair near the service road. I wait in the warm August air for Maman and Papa to come and pick her up.

I watch an early lunch trolley on the winding sidewalk below, being pushed along on clattering wheels past the trees and the summer lawns from the big kitchen in the main building toward the infirmary.

A group of male patients, all of them my age or a little older, comes out of Jack Hawking's cottage. They make their way over to the dining hall. Jack isn't among them.

Finally I see our car. Papa parks it near the children's pavilion just down the road. I watch Maman, and him, get out and close the car doors.

Maman straightens her pale summer dress and places her black purse, just so, over her arm. She is wearing a pretty hat I have never seen before. Papa buttons his jacket over his shirt, adjusts his old green fedora with the feather on the brim. I have not seen him since Christmas. He's put on a little weight. So, I notice, has Maman.

They don't see me. I don't call out to them. I feel as if I am spying on my own family. They walk up the road, then up the steps to the front door of the building, and go inside. Not long after, they walk out again, down the steps, and onto the road, with Josée between them.

She's looking up at them, holding their hands, wearing a brand-new blue dress with a big bow tied in her glossy hair. My heart stops. I wish, for just one moment, that it were me between Maman and Papa—them looking down at me in adoration, their beautiful child.

A nurse abruptly comes out of the building, calls to my family, and points up the road in my direction. I wave both arms. Josée sees me and breaks away, the satin bow slipping out of her hair. Behind her, Maman smiles and waves, and Papa leans over and snatches up the bow.

Josée is flying to me. Her legs have grown so long— she is such a gangly girl! Just as she reaches me, I see Papa straighten, take Maman's hand, lift it, and press her fingers to his lips.

Josée scrambles up into the wheelchair and throws her arms around my neck.

"When are you coming home?" Her breath is sweet in my ear.

I hug her tight.

"Not for a while," I whisper.

She pulls away and puts her hands on my cheeks, holding my head still, looking at me intently.

"I have to get well first," I tell her.

"Promise you'll come home soon?"

"I can't promise it will be soon, Josée."

"Why not?"

There is so much I want to say to her. Where do I even begin?

Then she says, "Guess what, Marie-Claire! Papa says there are baby ducks swimming in our slough! I'll see them today!"

Maman reaches me before Papa does.

"Hello, my girl," she says, brushing her fingers against my cheek.

I turn my eyes away from my sister and ask bluntly, "Where have you been?"

Maman crouches beside my wheelchair and turns her eyes in appeal to Papa. He leans in and lifts Josée into his arms.

"Do you think you are still able to sit on my shoulders?"

She shrieks with delight as he hoists her up onto his shoulders. She clutches his head. Knocks off his hat.

"Bring that along, will you?" he says to Maman.

And to me, the first words he has spoken in months, "Take care, Marie-Claire. You are always in our . . ."

His voice breaks off. He mops his face with one hand, his other holding Josée, turns with her, and shambles like a bear down the road.

I swipe angry tears from my own eyes. Maman takes both my hands in hers. I do not want to look at her. She makes me.

"Marie-Claire," she says, "it's hard for us all—but for him especially."

"To do what? To come and visit me and sit like a stupid man with his stupid hat in his hands and look at his stupid feet? That's all I would ask. Why does he hate me, Maman?"

"He doesn't hate you! Listen to me, he looks at you and he sees Luc. He sees Gérard. He sees how he's . . . failed to protect his family."

She nods. Seems about to say something else. Then, "I'm so sorry . . ." as her voice trails tearfully away.

I can see that I'm breaking her heart. It'll be a relief for her to join Papa and Josée, to get in the car and drive off and escape from having to deal with my awful questions. So I should just let her go. That would be the mature thing to do. Yet somehow I can't.

"So you're just going to leave me now, is that it? And come back in three or four weeks, and nothing's changed. Don't you even want to know how I'm doing? Can't you see I'm getting better? I'm in a new building. Nobody dies in this building, Maman. Don't you even want to know about it?"

"Marie-Claire, Papa and I . . . I'm pregnant."

"You're what?"

"Yes, yes it's true." She slides her eyes away; color

rushes up her cheeks. "Four months along. The baby will come in December. I haven't been so well. That's why it's been hard to get here."

"So it wasn't a cold. You lied to me."

"I'm better now. I'm much stronger. I feel like myself again. And now that you are no longer infectious with your TB, I'll come every week to see you, as I did before. I promise you."

In between having me and Luc and Josée, Maman had four miscarriages—and one other child, just after Josée, who was stillborn. What will happen to this one?

"Be happy for us all, Marie-Claire. This child is a blessing from God, an answer to our prayers. We've—every one of us—been so . . ."

Does she really think this is the answer to our prayers? Some new mouth to feed? Someone to replace Luc?

"I have to go now," she says, getting to her feet, picking up Papa's fedora.

Turning to me again, her eyes filling with a tenderness I cannot return, she says, "You look so much better, I can see that. Soon you'll come home, just like Josée. It's true, you will. I can see it in your face. And that will be such a happy day. But for now, I'll see you next Sunday."

"Don't bother."

Even though she offers her cheek to me, I turn my face away and don't kiss her goodbye. My insides gaping with loneliness, I watch her go down the road to join Papa and

165

Josée, who are now in the car, waiting to go home. Her shiny hair bounces under her hat and, yes, I can see now where she has thickened through the middle, just beginning to show signs of this ridiculous pregnancy.

After they drive off, I wait for the orderly, but no one comes. Evidently he's forgotten me, too. So I stand up. I've had enough of this wheelchair.

"Like some damn invalid," I say out loud. "Damn it to hell, anyway."

"Hello, Marie-Claire."

I whirl around. It's Jack Hawkings, and he's looking like I'm the funniest thing he's ever seen.

I fall back into the wheelchair. He comes around to face me.

He says, losing his smile, "Didn't mean to startle you, honest to God."

"I'm having a terrible morning."

This wasn't how I thought I'd see him again. In this awful faille dress, after my family has abandoned me.

I start to cry. Only it's something beyond crying. It goes from crying to sobbing to something else. To making sounds I've never made before.

Between the noises, I tell him, "I'm sorry . . . to be such an idiot."

He hunkers down beside the wheelchair, places his hand on my arm, pats it awkwardly.

"Some days are worse than others in this place," he

says. "It's hard to keep up appearances. You don't have to do it on my account."

It's a relief to hear someone say this. "They brought me out here to . . . I said goodbye to my little . . . to my sister . . ."

He digs into his pocket, takes out a folded handkerchief, and hands it to me.

"Here, it's clean."

"Oh . . . thank you . . ."

I take his handkerchief and press it to my face. It's cool and soft.

I manage to stop crying.

"It's a beautiful day," he says. "I think you could use a walk. Do you want me to take you?"

"Please."

Please, please, get me out of here.

"Good then."

Grabbing the handles of the wheelchair, he pushes me down the road, veering off across the sloping lawn and onto the sidewalk. We lurch along past a lunch trolley, nearly hitting it.

The orderly shouts, "Watch out!"

Jack stops, salutes him, leaves me, grabs chicken legs, buns, fruit, and napkins from the trolley, comes back, and throws it all in my lap.

Now I'm laughing.

The orderly yells after us, "Hey! What do you think you're doing? Come back here with that!"

But we're gone, flying down the sidewalk behind the main building, and next thing, we're heading for a glade of trees.

"I hope you like picnics," says Jack, out of breath. I hear a TB wheeze.

"Pneumo," he adds. "Right lung."

"Me, too, right side. We match."

"Sometimes"—he slows down—"I forget I'm sick. I just play out more than usual."

We reach the trees, their umbrella of light and shade, away from spying eyes.

Sounds of laughter and conversation come from the screened-in veranda off the dining hall on the second floor of the main building, patients and staff eating at tables in the summer air.

I stand up. Jack takes the blanket from my chair and spreads it on the grass. We sit, and he leans back on his elbows, still a bit out of breath, and looks over at me.

I notice for the first time that his eyes are brown and have a deep sparkle. I think about his kiss on the night of the kite, the way it felt like a hot star falling on my palm—and I blush and have to look away.

We start to eat our picnic lunch. A couple of minutes go by in which I don't know what to say to him.

"I've got something to show you," he says, as if whatever it is, is the most important thing to talk about.

He dusts his hands on his napkin, pulls a wallet from his back pocket, slides out a photograph, and passes it over.

It's been taken twenty or so years before, of a young woman who leans against a porch railing, arms and legs lovely and graceful, as if she could walk right out of the picture and sit down on the blanket with us.

"An early photo of my mother, Sheila."

"She's beautiful."

"She died a year ago . . . of TB," he says, still looking at the photo. "Sure makes you grow up quick, doesn't it, losing people like that. I used to think it was best not to make friends in a place like this. No guarantees anybody's going to make it out of here, right?"

I don't say anything. All those months with Signy, and now here I am sitting with him—with this handsome boy who watched my brother die.

"You never know what's going to happen, though, to change your mind about things," Jack goes on. "I mean, when I couldn't go to my own mother's funeral, when I was too sick with TB even to manage that, I felt good and goddamn lost. After that my roommate died a miserable death. I guess you might say that in his final days, when he could really have used a friend, I let him down. Anyway, finally, along comes summer and I'm out on the balcony and I just want to be left alone. Somebody comes to visit me—a chaplain . . ."

I grab his arm. "You mean Fred? Carries around an old deck of cards?"

He does a double take, grins. "That's the guy!"

"Thinks he's a magician."

I tell him about Fred coming to visit me on the infirmary balcony—and the queens of hearts he seemed to produce out of the air.

"They were everywhere. Popping out of my book, flying off the window screen. I found one under my pillow. I still have them, three of them. They kind of feel like . . . wishes."

"Yeah? What kind of wishes?"

I feel foolish for having said it.

"Come on, be honest. What have you wished lately?"

"Most of my wishes have to do with getting out of this place," I finally tell him.

"I'm with you on that one." He leans in and whispers playfully, "Fred also plays a mean hand of crazy eights."

I laugh. "Crazy eights?"

"Yep, first couple of Sundays when he came by, he completely skunked me. So there's this little competitive streak in me that starts to come alive again. By the sixth Sunday I realize I'm lying there waiting to see him, in fact I'm counting on it! He stopped by a lot of Sundays after that, and he never once shoved God in my face. We just played cards, and that was it. Come to think of it, it probably took a lot of courage for him to be with me. I was in bad shape, sick as a dog and really ticked off about everything—not exactly a barrel of laughs to be with. Anyway, I finally started to recover. Then I noticed Robert and Sandy. We got to be friends, and I stopped acting like such a phony-baloney stoic. I still have my moments, though."

He picks a blade of grass, twirls it between his fingers. "How about your friend Signy? That must have been hard for you to leave her behind in the infirmary. Is she real sick?"

I don't answer. I don't know what to say.

"I'll take you over there if you like. To visit her, I mean. And—from my own experience—don't leave it too long."

I dread going back to that place. With its reminders of our torn-apart family, and how sick we all were, and Luc and Gérard. Every step down those halls carries an echo of the dark months.

Jack reaches over to show me more photos. Of his sister, Lorna, "She's fourteen, the baby." And his brother, Ted, "Off being an air force pilot. I think I remember mentioning him to you, because he's the one I was telling Luc about . . ."

He stops, nods his head, looks away, caught off guard somehow, and adds softly, "Yeah, so this is my brother."

I stare at Ted—smiling and handsome in his uniform—yet not so handsome, to my way of thinking, as Jack. I get the same feeling from his picture as I did from Signy's Sebastian. Too sure of himself, maybe. I hand back the picture and look into Jack's face and say nothing.

"Unlike my brother, I couldn't get in," Jack says.

"Tried to enlist, and they didn't want me. I'd had pleurisy, and that was a problem. By then I'd quit school and got in with this dance band. We were traveling all over the country entertaining the boys in training, not to mention the people they'd be leaving behind, so I guess it was an important thing to do. That's what we told ourselves, anyway. We were doing our bit for the war effort."

"It must have been fun, too," I say, thinking about all the dances I've never been to.

"It was okay at first. Exciting, even. But making music is a hard life, Marie-Claire. I found that out pretty quick. One town after another, trying to sleep at the back of a tour bus, forgetting to eat. I didn't drink, and most of the guys were hard drinkers. And I didn't chase after girls—although there were plenty of opportunities. I'm just old-fashioned enough not to be interested in one-night stands, and when you're touring around the country in a bus, that's about all you're going to get. I wanted something more. So I guess you could say I was the odd man out there, too."

"So why didn't you just quit?"

"Easier said than done. I got trapped inside the life. Stubborn pride, didn't know what else to do. Wanted to prove a point, I guess—wanted to make it on my own, without any help from dear old Dad. Anyway, pretty soon the rest of the musicians started to joke around and call me the Saint. I'd laugh it off and sit at the back of the bus sketching pictures of them. I've still got a big sketchbook filled with pictures of those guys and the scenes I saw out the bus windows—I can show it to you sometime, if you like. It was a lonely life, not glamorous like some people think. I started to lose weight and cough, and next thing you know, this pleurisy I'd had turns up again, only as TB . . . Funny thing, I was almost grateful for it . . . almost . . ."

A bird settles in the branches just over our heads. We both turn to look at it and our eyes meet.

I feel grateful for this little moment—just to be sitting here with Jack—for us both to be alive today. I want to tell him so, yet I don't know how that would sound. Just like that, out loud.

Instead I reach over and take his hand. He looks at my hand in his, looks at me, and leans in. I think, he's going to kiss me! Then he does, his lips soft and hot on my mouth. He holds the kiss. A flowering of sparks moves through my body. He pulls away. Looks at me in surprise, and pulls me onto his lap. He kisses me again, his lips breaking away to graze my cheek, my neck. I fold myself against him, clinging to him, my heart thudding wildly, my head on his shoulder, his hand stroking my hair, and the world just stops.

"Marie-Claire," he says at last, his voice thick, "maybe I should take you back."

I lift my head to look into his eyes. "Why? I'm in trouble already."

He laughs, bends to my ear, and whispers, "I think we both are."

173

— ♥ —

At the cottage we meet up with Annie. With a frantic wave she exclaims, "Where in God's green earth have you been with her? Mr. Hawkings, don't you have work detail right now? Aren't you supposed to be at the infirmary with the bedpans at this very minute?"

"I know. I'm sorry," he says, looking at his watch.

"Indeed you should be," she says, her hands on her hips.

"I'm sorry. We j-just . . ." I stammer, looking up at him.

Jack puts his hands on my shoulders, rests them there, and says, "I took very good care of her. She's had a bad morning."

"I know all about her morning, so don't give me any of your sauce," says Annie, piercing him with a look. "You'd better leave now. You'll need to get a pass to spend time with her."

"I'll be sure to do that."

He looks first at her, then at me, and winks. He mouths "see you" to me, just as Annie starts wrestling the awkward chair backward up to the cottage door.

"Saucy monkey, he is," she mutters.

"We just had a picnic," I tell her. I feel like I'm floating.

"Right, a picnic, and I'm the queen of England."

TWENTY-ONE

August 19, 1942. That's a date people will remember. Canadians, especially. It was awful. A battle in France, at a place called Dieppe. At first the newspapers and radio reports call it a great victory. Later a different story starts to leak out. There are, in fact, more bodies than can at first be counted—young men from small towns and big cities all over Canada. Big black government cars, with their terrible news, keep pulling up to people's doorsteps, we are told. Children left fatherless, mothers and fathers grieving.

Annie comes to get me. I have just woken up. I can't get into my head who wants to see me.

"Your father," she repeats. "By himself. Get up now. Here's your robe. Just slip it on. He's waiting outside. He seems upset."

As she's helping me into the sleeves, I think, something

has happened to Maman! Or to this baby she's carrying. Or maybe to Josée! I pull the tie around my robe and stumble frantically into my slippers.

"I'll help you into the chair," Annie says.

"I don't need a wheelchair."

She stands back, gives me the eye.

"I'm strong enough, Annie."

I want him to see for himself that I'm getting better.

She reluctantly leaves. I walk out into the hall and down to the cottage door.

There is Papa on the other side, hat in his hand, waiting for me.

"Who is sick?"

"No one," he answers, and adds, in a blustery way, "I've come . . . to tell you something."

"Okay," I say, wondering what he could possibly have to say to me.

There's a bench outside the cottage. I ease down at one end, while he sits at the other. I gather my hands in my lap and wait for him to speak.

First he surprises me by putting his arm along the back of the bench, just as he used to do when he was teaching me how to drive the car in our cow pasture.

"It's been a bad time, very bad for people," he says at last, and I know he's talking about Dieppe.

I think about Joe and how he couldn't wait for something to finally happen over in Europe. I wonder whether I'll ever know if he was at Dieppe.

The August wind stirs the oak leaves high above us.

Papa says, "The Berard brothers, Marius and Guy. Both dead."

I lift my head in awful surprise. Marius Berard—the boy who, when we were nine, gave me that first insulting kiss. Marius, dead at sixteen, and Guy at eighteen.

Papa's face is gray as he lowers his head and looks at his feet. With a great sigh, he adds, "Your friend Yvette . . ."

"Yvette LaBossière? What's happened?"

"To Yvette, nothing. She's still living somewhere in Winnipeg, they say."

He won't say out loud that she was pregnant when she left St. Felix.

"It's her brother, Marie-Claire," he says quietly. "Marc."

"Marc? Marc LaBossière?"

"Missing in action. Thought to be dead."

I think about Marc on the day I sneaked out and met Joe at the dance. Marc, that Saturday, coming up to Yvette and me outside Drapeau's. Carrying his four-year-old, Angela, like a sack of potatoes under his big golden arm, telling us proudly that he'd just enlisted. Marc, who taught me to skate . . .

"Of course one hopes . . ." Papa gulps for air. "How can God let this happen?"

"But how will his family manage without him?"

He waves his hand around, catching sunlight and shadows, watching them on his skin. He drops his arm,

177

sits back like a man whose heart is breaking. "And yet we go on. Yes, we must go on."

He's thinking about Luc. Maybe that's why he came today.

A few more seconds go by as he alternately pats and paws at the space on the bench between us.

"Marie-Claire," he continues, "I should never have let Gérard come and live with us. All of my children . . ." he adds, just above a whisper. He drops his head, shakes it.

I wait for him to say more. But with this he sighs, puts his hands on his knees, and stands.

I also get to my feet.

I am surprised as, with great dignity, he offers me his arm—a kind of peace offering, perhaps. Still, I don't take it. He drops his arm and turns and looks at me, and I look back and hold him in my gaze.

"It wasn't Gérard's fault," I tell him slowly. "Do you honestly think he would knowingly have brought TB to us? That's a monstrous idea—none of us knew! And Papa, it wasn't your fault, either. It really wasn't. People just die for no good reason, and bad things happen and will keep on happening."

There is a look of shock on his face, as if I have slapped him. Right after, he recovers, reaches out his hand, and awkwardly squeezes my shoulder. And quickly turns and does his bear-shamble down the road, still carrying the weight of the world that he always seems to think he has to have on his shoulders.

Five years of this . . . of saying goodbye to people.
It's hard for people to visit . . . I know that . . .

I call out, "Papa!"

He stumbles, rights himself, and turns to me again.

"Tell Maman and Josée . . ."

What? There they'll be when he gets back to the farm, Josée sitting at the table, no brother and no sister, not like it was before and never will be again. Maman pregnant, but knowing, even though she told me, "This child is an answer to our prayers," that another life can never replace Luc's. And Papa in a state of misery for all that has been lost to him—yes, misery, I see it now, see it plainly on his face—even misery at the thought of losing me.

I can't just send him away like this.

"Tell them," I say, "tell Maman and Josée that I send my love. Please give them that message for me, Papa."

He smiles broadly, just beams as if I have given him the best present in the world.

"Yes, yes, I'll tell them that," he says. "I'll tell them you send your love, Marie-Claire."

Today is the fourth of September, and I haven't yet gone back to visit Signy. Her old roommate, Louise, waited five months before she finally came for a visit. On the day she was discharged, no less. It's only been a couple of weeks. Well, more like two and a half, but today I'm going back to the land of TB exiles to see her, I'm definitely doing it.

The good news is that Annie's finally agreed to let me

see Jack—even if it is only to take me over to the west infirmary and bring me back again.

I'm wearing a short-sleeved sweater and a plaid skirt that Annie found for me in a box of cast-off clothes. I sit on the bench outside Creighton Cottage and wait for him.

There he is! I get to my feet and wave madly. He's wearing hospital whites. He quickly walks across the road to me.

"What, no wheelchair? Guess you don't need me, then!" he teases.

I practically fly into his arms. He smells so good. He feels so good. I put my own arms around him and lean all against him as he kisses me.

"I can't believe that Annie," I say, as I pull back for air and smile into his eyes. "Arranging for you to take me over there, isn't that nice?"

He throws back his head and laughs. His whole face crinkles up, and it's bewitching. "I figured she didn't want me around you, period—dear God, sixteen days! It's been torture."

"For me, too. Torture." I roll my eyes and flirt with him and feel so happy.

He laughs again, tucking my hand into the crook of his arm.

Nurse Thompson is the first person I see in the west infirmary. Jack has stopped a little way back to tie his shoe.

"How is she?" I ask.

She lowers her voice. "Struggling more than usual. Don't let her see that on your face. Keep it light."

"I would have been here sooner," I say lamely. "Annie wanted me to . . . to get settled first. Aren't there rules about how often I can visit?"

"Yes, there are—but rules, Marie-Claire, are not always prudent or particularly useful. Signy needs to see you. So please tell Annie for me that any time you want to visit, you're welcome. It's not going to hurt you a bit. It'll be good for you, in fact. And it will certainly be good for Signy."

With a nod, as Jack catches up, she says, "Nice to see you both," turns, and hurries into her office.

Signy is turned away from us deep in her bed under the covers as we walk onto the balcony. Mrs. McTigg waves a knitting needle at me. I give her a little wave back. She says nothing but casts a look at Signy. Her mouth goes into a tight line of concern. My heart sinks.

I don't know what I expected. For sure, I didn't expect her to be worse.

Jack hangs back at the doorway of the balcony as I sit on the side of Signy's bed. Her hair needs cutting. I reach out and touch her shoulder.

With a quick intake of breath, she wakes, turns over, and looks up at me like I'm a stranger.

"Hi," I say.

She looks over and sees Jack, says nothing.

"Hi," he says to her, and to me, "I'm wanted over at

the east infirmary. I'll be back to collect you in an hour. Nice seeing you, Signy."

He leaves, and I look back at her. She's lost more weight. I can see it in her face. And she's flushed—struggling with TB fevers again.

"I'm sorry I didn't get here sooner," I tell her.

"Oh." That's all she says.

She's in a mess. I can plainly see this.

I tell her cheerfully, "I read that article you told me about. You know, the one in *Life* magazine? The one about the Andrews Sisters entertaining the troops?"

I wait for her to respond. When she doesn't, I try something else.

"Remember the night you got that radio station to play one of their songs for me? 'Boogie Woogie Bugle Boy'? That's a nice song."

"So you're with Jack now," she says flatly.

"Y-yes."

"Guess you've been busy."

With that, she rolls over and gives me her back again. I'm here to be with her, and yet, sick as she is, I think she'd like me to leave.

Yet I can't just up and leave, so I sit and wait instead. I'm still sitting, waiting, when Jack comes back for me an hour later—appearing at the door of the balcony, leaning tall against the archway.

Signy's breathing more evenly. Maybe she's fallen asleep. I get up from the bed and quietly go.

Jack and I walk back outside into the sunlight. He takes my hand. I feel raw inside.

"She's not doing too well," he says.

"No, she isn't," I admit. "Can you come by tomorrow afternoon, after cure hour?"

He squeezes my hand. "I'll be here."

I go inside, walk onto the balcony. Rose, cutting her toenails, looks over, sizing me up.

"So how was your visit?"

All she's doing is looking for gossip.

I don't answer and head for the bathroom.

Julie's in there, leaning against the sink, gazing at her tired face in the mirror.

She turns and watches me put the plug in the tub, turn the water on full blast. I feel exhausted and sick and miserable, my TB bugs firmly in control. I haul off the sweater, the skirt, my underpants with the elastic that's going, and so on. I stumble into the tub. Julie comes to stand over me with a bottle of shampoo in her hand. She pours some under the spout.

"Bubbles," she explains, as fragrant froth starts to billow around me.

She pulls up a chair to sit beside me, watches for a minute, then strips off her pajamas and gets in with me at the opposite end of the tub.

"Never waste a good bubble bath," she says, sinking back, lifting a leg to examine her toenail polish before lowering her foot into the water again.

"Signy's in bad shape," I tell her.

Julie leans her head back against the tub rim, lifts it, gives me a look, and then lolls back again.

Silence, except for the dripping tap.

"You're a good person, Marie-Claire."

"What's that supposed to mean?"

She's quiet for a moment, lifts her head again, looks all around her. "Aren't these bubbles pretty? Don't you just love bubble baths?"

"I do, thanks," I mumble, sinking down into the hot bath.

TWENTY-TWO

Tuesday morning Miss Neustadt, our teacher, comes to see Julie and me, rolling her big black chalkboard on its squeaky wheels onto the balcony.

"Good morning, girls," she says.

I've missed so much school. Now, on this warm September day, classes with Sister Thérèse seem long ago.

Rose, who has a head cold and isn't performing her usual duties at the main building as a Hello Girl, listens in. She sneezes and blows her nose incessantly and loudly, and does what she can to give off signals that we're disturbing her with our learning.

I tune her out like she's radio static.

At the end of the hour, Miss Neustadt advises, "Personally, I'd get as much education as I can if I were you, girls. I spent a year as a secretary, hated it, contracted TB, chased the cure, and finished my degree while I was still in bed. And here I am teaching. It isn't such a bad life."

"You mean somebody like me could get a degree . . . here at the San?" I venture.

"We hope you don't have TB that long, Marie-Claire."

Miss Neustadt throws me a smile and hurries off with her blackboard.

After she's gone I stare past the balcony screens at the leaves that are chattering in the wind.

Rose, sitting on top of her blankets, feet crossed at the ankles, surrounded by crumpled snotty tissues, flips through a *Silver Screen* magazine. She sneezes before she says, "You don't want that, do you?"

I slowly turn my head. "Want what?"

"Some fancy degree. What would you do with it?"

"Maybe," I say, barely above a whisper, "I just want it."

"Crazy, if you ask me." Rose stops, as if lost in thought. "Have I told you girls that they might give me a leave at Christmas?"

Julie lifts her head from her pillow to glare at her. "You mean they'd actually let you out of here?"

"I'm so much farther ahead of the rest of you," Rose goes on, happily examining her fingernails. "I'll probably be gone for seven days."

"We'll miss your sparkling personality," Julie tells her.

In the afternoon Jack stops by just as he said he would. We hold each other for a long time. The air is sweet and heavy with the promise of rain.

"I brought you something," he says, after we finally break away. "Put out your hand."

I do, and he places, right in the middle of my palm, the thing that I thought was gone forever.

The silver chain, and the St. Christopher's medal with the heart beside it. A bit tarnished, yet looking pretty much like it did the day I gave it to Oncle Gérard.

"How did you get this?" I say, looking up at him.

"Fred the chaplain gave it to me."

"Fred gave it to you?"

"It was given to him by a patient who knew he was dying. Hope you don't mind how I got it."

"But why . . . ?"

"I was feeling quite hopeless, and Fred told me the guy who gave it to him thought it might help someone else. You were pretty down yesterday."

"Thank you!"

I slip it over my head, feeling medal and chain and heart warm against my skin. Sometime I'll tell him about it, but not right now. I clutch the medal with one hand and find his hand with the other. They fit, our hands, as if they've always belonged.

When we reach the west infirmary, and the balcony, Jack smiles over my shoulder at Signy, and the lightness of our mood dissolves.

"Be back in an hour. You two have a nice visit," he says quietly, and disappears into the hallway.

I turn and brace myself as I ease down to sit beside her. Her every movement seems to be an effort.

All at once, I'm remembering how it felt, that tiredness when I hardly had even the strength to lift a spoon.

"Do you feel like hell?" I ask her. And then, "Of course you do. You're a mess."

She stares at the unfamiliar necklace hanging from my neck, looks away, and says, "I missed you."

"Well, I'm here now."

"I'm tired of fighting to get better."

What am I supposed to say to that? What do I do?

"How about a back rub?"

Without a word, she rolls over and lets me undo the ties of her gown.

"How come you're wearing this?" I ask. "What happened to your nice pajamas and bed jackets? Why have they put you in this horrible thing?"

"I don't know. Maybe it's easier . . ."

For her? For the staff? But I don't say anything.

I draw back her gown and see the long thoracoplasty scar. From a distance I'd always thought it was just one scar, when actually, there are three jagged ones that almost—yet don't quite—join up. I'm not sure I really want to touch her, but I do anyway, and begin to drift my fingers over the scars.

Suddenly she rolls over again, looks up at me with her eyes all red, and says, "You don't have to do this."

"Do what?"

"This," she hisses. "Coming to see me. Pretending to be my friend. Like it's . . . it's your obligation or something."

She grasps the blankets and pulls them up around her, her hands trembling from the effort.

I find my voice, just barely. "But I am your friend, Signy."

Silence. "I don't want your pity, Marie-Claire. I don't want your charity. If you can't be a real friend to me, then just go away."

She closes her eyes, shutting me out.

I look over at Mrs. McTigg, who is furiously knitting. Her face is scarlet.

When Jack comes to get me, I'm standing out in the hallway, leaning against the wall. He's been whistling happily as he comes along. He notices me and stops.

"What's up?"

"Let's get out of here," I say, pushing past him.

He follows me speedily down the hall and out of the building and finally catches up on the sidewalk—reaching out for my arm, making me stop, turning me to face him.

"We had a fight," I explain, meeting his gaze.

"A fight? Is that all?" His shoulders sag with relief. "I thought it was something really bad."

I flare up. "It *was* really bad, Jack."

"She isn't dying, is she?"

I look at him coldly. "No." I just want to be left alone. I walk away from him again.

"What have I done? Marie-Claire?"

I keep walking and don't look back.

Julie is the first person I see when I return to Creighton Cottage. She's standing in the front hall, dressed in regular clothes.

"Hi," she says happily. "Annie let me go outside for a walk, and it's such a beautiful day. I just got back. How's Signy?"

"She doesn't want to see me anymore," I mutter.

"Oh my God, did you two have a fight?"

I nod. It's all starting to sink in. Shock and hurt, yes, that's what I feel. Mainly shame, though, and it's the shame that's the worst. It digs like a prickly thing into my heart and won't let go.

I don't want your charity. If you can't be a real friend to me, then just go away.

TWENTY-THREE

On Wednesday I drag myself over to the infirmary for fluoroscopy, X-ray, and more air on my lung.

"You're doing really well, Marie-Claire," Dr. Yuen says. "You've put on more weight. Your TB cavity has shrunk dramatically. We're going to increase your activity. I want you to take two half-hour walks every day—wherever you like, as long as it's still on the grounds. And you can also start going over to the dining hall for your evening meals."

Just like that! More freedom, all at once, than in the nine months since I came here.

"Oh yes," he adds, "and think about what you'd like to do for your work-up program. By Christmas, or a little after, you'll probably be fit enough to start."

So I'm getting better, dramatically better.

"Is there something else you want to talk about, Marie-Claire?"

"Oh, y-yes, well," I stammer. "I'm just wondering, you know, how long . . . I'll be here."

He says sympathetically, "It's really hard to tell. I can't say, but a while longer."

"A while? How long is a while?"

"Another six months, at the very least. Probably more."

"More?"

"You were a very sick girl when you came to us. And yes, you've made remarkable progress, but this stuff can come back at you, Marie-Claire. I'm not saying it will. Just that we need to keep you chasing the cure until we feel your disease is arrested and you're truly out of the woods."

I leave the conference room and don't feel like going back to Creighton Cottage. I could force myself to take a walk, but where do you go when you feel that there's no place you belong in the world?

Then I do walk. One step leads to another.

Before I know it, I'm in the west infirmary.

Mrs. Thompson is standing at the front desk, setting up a tray of tiny brown glass bottles and large needles. When she sees me, she looks grave. "I know you've come to see Signy. Maybe not today."

"What?" I say, my mouth going dry. "What's wrong?"

She nods at her feet, looks up again. "She had a little episode yesterday afternoon. Just after you left, actually."

"Episode?"

"A bleed. We're keeping a very close eye on her. We need to keep her calm."

I head for the balcony.

Mrs. Thompson comes after me and cuts me off. She's holding the tray in one hand. The other she places firmly on my arm.

"She's back in her room," she says. "And she needs absolute quiet, Marie-Claire. I'm going to have to ask you to respect that."

She drops her hand and heads down the hallway, the skirts of her starched uniform rustling, her white shoes squeaking over the linoleum.

I watch as she walks into one of the rooms. Then I march right down to the room that Signy and I once shared.

It's very dim. A small wind from the open window puffs out the curtains, which are partway closed. Signy, in the middle of the bed, her head and shoulders and chest propped up by pillows, lies very still.

Her eyes are open and they follow me. I pull up a chair. As I sit, she makes a small motion, as if to turn away. It seems that if she had the strength to get up and run from me, she would.

"Please be still," I whisper. "I don't want to make you feel worse, and I won't stay long."

I bow my head, but I still feel her eyes on me—their accusation.

"I came," I tell her finally, "to say I'm sorry. For . . . for ignoring you."

She says nothing. The wind continues to buffet the curtains. In the hallway, someone rattles past the door with a trolley.

"I just got caught up with this and that."

Excuses, excuses. This isn't what she wants to hear.

"I'm so sorry, Signy. And I . . . I want you to get better."

"Why?" she asks at last.

That's all, just why.

"Don't talk, okay? Let me tell you something."

What do I tell her?

She closes her eyes, yet I feel she is listening, and now I have to say the right things.

"Do you remember the day we met, Signy? You seemed so damn cheerful. And I was so . . . scared and angry. You talked to me, even when I didn't want you to. You kept talking through all the things that happened— how sick I was and my pneumo and Papa never coming to visit and Maman so scared for all of her kids that I don't think she saw me even when she did visit. And Luc— when he died. And then all the months we chased the cure together. We were bored and sick and . . . I cut your hair. Do you remember that day? You said how much fun it was. Did you know the whole time how scared I was that I might make you sicker? But it *was* fun. And even when I was grumpy with you . . . those times . . . you never stopped, not even once stopped trying to be a friend to me. So now you have to keep trying to get well, Signy. I mean it."

I get up to leave. "I'll be by tomorrow, okay?"

She slowly turns her head on her pillows and looks at

me one last time. And I don't know if she wants me around, or not.

On Thursday afternoon I find Jack outside Creighton Cottage, waiting to see me.

"Look," he says, with a frown. "I still don't know what I've done. Whatever it is, I'm sorry, okay?"

"There's nothing to forgive," I tell him. "Signy's having a bad time, and I have to be a better friend to her."

"But you've been visiting her," he says, surprised. "You are a good friend."

I give him a look. He holds up his hands. "Let's not fight."

"Okay," I say with a little laugh.

He smiles, shakes his head, and looks down at his feet, then back at me again. "Julie's been keeping Robert and me up to date. Guess you girls have both got dining hall privileges. That's a step in the right direction."

I take a breath. "I want to go over to see Signy, on my own."

"On your own," he repeats. "Okay. I'll be around . . . if you need anything."

He walks away, his shoulders sagging with disappointment.

There's no one in the hallway when I come to visit Signy. The door to our old room is almost all the way closed, and I push it slowly open.

She seems weaker than yesterday. Can't even seem to open her eyes. One hand lies still on top of the covers. I sit beside her, take her hand, and hold it lightly.

Several minutes pass. Nurse Thompson comes into the room. I brace myself, but she doesn't tell me to leave. Instead she moves to the other side of the bed and places a tray of needles and bottles on the bedside table. She gently swabs Signy's arm with alcohol. Administers a shot.

After that she says in a tight voice, "Her parents are away right now and can't be reached. I'm glad she has you."

I hold Signy's hand through the rest of the afternoon. Until I don't know how long I've been here, except that, beyond the windows of the room we used to share, the sun is slipping down.

As I get up to go, just as I'm releasing her hand, I feel it flutter in mine. I stand beside her for a while, leaning into the bed, feeling like I'm going to fall to pieces.

At last, I leave.

I've missed supper in the dining hall. Julie is the only one back in bed when I come onto the balcony. She seems to have caught Rose's cold and looks dragged out and tired.

"We missed you at supper," she says.

"Signy's not good—at all."

"Ohhh, I'm so sorry."

"Yes," I say in a small voice.

I lie on my bed, kick off my shoes and, fully dressed,

pull the covers over me. I'm swimming with exhaustion. And, finally, tears.

Julie says, "Jack's worried about you. We all are."

I'm too tired to reply. I cover my head with the blankets, and then I sleep.

On Friday morning when I wake up, the first face I see in my mind is Signy's. Now all I want to do is go to her. Through breakfast and morning lessons with Miss Neustadt, I think about her. Finally afternoon comes and I hurry to the infirmary, to its smells of sickness. I come up the hall and meet Nurse Thompson just as she's about to go into Signy's room.

"How is she?" I ask.

"It's a waiting game. I don't know what else to tell you, Marie-Claire. We simply don't know right now."

I go into the room and to Signy and take her hand. The minute I do, I feel a faint current, even though she hasn't moved a muscle. I sit, and after that, somehow, we both hold on fast.

TWENTY-FOUR

Saturday and Sunday I go to see Signy, and each time I hold her hand and feel her life. Sometimes it's faint, but I always find it, somehow.

By Monday, when I go to visit, her face is turned toward the door. Her eyes are open as I come into the room. I hurry over to her, sit down, and take her hand. I look into her eyes and nod my head. She closes her eyes again, and we start once more with this, whatever it is we are doing, this wordless spirit thing that's moving back and forth between us. All I know is I have to be here and we have to keep on doing it.

Mrs. Thompson appears, disappears. Dr. Yuen comes by. He stands and watches us for a while.

"How are you, Marie-Claire?" he asks at last.

"I'm fine," I tell him, not taking my eyes off Signy. "Just fine."

"Don't tire yourself out," he says, and then he leaves, too.

— ♥ —

Slowly, over the next few weeks, Signy improves. One day, when I come into her room at the end of week three, there she is, actually propped into a sitting position against the pillows. Her eyes are moving around the room like she's seeing it for the first time. Then she sees me, and smiles, and this makes me so happy that my heart almost stops.

I ease myself up beside her on the bed and find her pale waxy hand. We link fingers and sit that way for a while.

Later, when I'm saying goodbye for the day, she looks up at me, her eyes shining, and says, "Do you believe in miracles, Marie-Claire?"

I could tell her yes, but I don't know what I believe about miracles. I take her hand once more and shake it around a bit and then, because I can't think of what else to do, I reach inside the neckline of my sweater and pull the St. Christopher's medal over my head.

"This is part of me," I say. "I want you to have it."

"Oh," she says as I carefully lift her head and place it on her.

See You Soon

Christmas 1942

TWENTY-FIVE

One by one, Julie and I and Robert and Jack are told that we're being given a home leave at Christmas.

"Seven days of freedom! Can you believe it?" Julie's eyes shine with excitement. "And Robert's coming with me! He'll get to meet my grandparents! Oh, my granny will be so happy. We'll have a big family Christmas."

We're having lunch in the dining hall. Robert and Julie hold hands under the table. Jack pushes his food around on his plate.

"Are you going home?" I ask him.

"Sure," he says without enthusiasm. He sits back and looks at me. "Although Christmas is kind of a strange time now. How about you?"

"Yes. I know it's going to be different, but I really want to. Maman's pregnant, you know."

After we've eaten, Jack says, "Want to go for a walk?"

It's a sunny day. The trees are heavy with frost. The

ground glitters with snow. We wade through it and kick at the soft drifts like a couple of little kids.

In a while we stop, and Jack turns me to face him. We stand there looking into each other's eyes.

"I think I understand," he says. "You and me—who knows what will happen. But Signy, that's forever, right?"

I nod. He understands things better than I thought he did. Better than even I did.

"Forever maybe isn't very long—for Signy," I say.

"I know, believe me, I know that. It's why I haven't pushed things between you and me."

"Thank you," I say, tears welling up in my eyes.

"I'm a patient guy," he adds, with a smile.

"A patient patient."

We walk along like that for a while, each with our hands tucked for warmth inside our own pockets. Our shoulders almost touching.

At last he says, "Marie-Claire, I'm . . . I'm being discharged."

I stop and turn to him. "Discharged? Oh Jack, when?"

"End of January."

"That soon?"

"Here's the thing, though. I might stay on for a while. They need all the help they can get. Turns out I'm pretty good with patients. I'd live in staff quarters and work at the infirmary. We could . . . still see each other. But only if you want to."

"Yes," I say, walking into his arms.

— ♥ —

Signy's propped up in a chair in her room. The minute I come through the door, she says, "Look what my mum sent you and me on the train."

A steamer trunk sits on the floor at the end of her bed. The handles on either end are tied with big red satin bows that are bedraggled from all the handling and hauling around they've been through since leaving the city.

"Why the bows?"

"Early Christmas present for us both," Signy says mysteriously. "Want to open it?"

I slide the trunk over until it's closer to her. Then I unlock and raise the lid.

Signy claps her hands and laughs. "She's sent us what I wanted!"

Her mother has been to visit maybe three or four times since last Christmas. She didn't even bother to show up when she got back from her trip, wherever the hell she went, after Signy was so sick and needed to see her.

Anyway, Signy's beautiful rich mother has managed to get together a trunk, stuffed right to the brim with lovely things. Signy keeps softly exclaiming as we lift up each item and lay it across her bed.

"Oh, look at this! Oh, and this!"

There are quilted satin dressing gowns, pajamas and slippers, sweaters in all textures and colors, slacks, skirts, dresses for every occasion, blouses both frilled and tailored,

stockings, socks, underwear, jackets, shoes, and boots—
everything for fall and winter. Plus two woolen coats with
matching scarves, tams, and mittens.

"Where did she get all this?" I ask.

"Oh, I know what you mean. What with the war going
on and the stores so empty these days, I'm not sure. Even
with all of her connections. This is more than even I expected. Try on your coat. It's the royal red one."

I ease my arms into a coat that's a deep red, like
Christmas itself. It warms quickly against my skin.

"Do you like it, Marie-Claire?"

I don't know what to say. I start to think about the fact
that the other coat is obviously for her, for Signy, and
when will she ever get to wear it?

"You look beautiful," Signy says, reaching out her
arms. "And you'll be warm."

As I hug her, feeling how heartbreakingly fragile she
still is, she whispers, "My mother's so grateful to you.
She's happy we're friends. All this stuff—it's just her way,
Marie-Claire."

I don't take off the red coat even though it's hot in the
room. The radiator hisses and leaks rusty water, just the
same as it did last winter. Nobody's bothered to fix it.
Sweat starts to trickle down my back.

"Your folks coming to visit you again this Christmas?"
I ask, trying to keep my voice light.

"Oh well," Signy says, not meeting my eyes. "It's only
one day."

What does that mean? Does it mean they're coming, or not? And even if they are, she's right.

What's one day, when there are three hundred sixty-four others in which to feel you've pretty much been abandoned.

TWENTY-SIX

On December 22, 1942, the day after my seventeenth birthday, I'm in Creighton Cottage's cramped kitchen, wrapping handmade Christmas gifts.

Rose sticks her head into the room. Her hair is tied up in tight rag curlers in anticipation of the holidays and her leave in Winnipeg.

"Call for you," she says.

She follows me to the telephone on the hall table just outside the kitchen. My heart thuds as I pick up the receiver. People don't call me. I turn my back. Rose will, of course, stand there the whole time and listen in.

I'm so afraid of bad news.

"Hello?" I say shakily.

Papa's voice comes booming over the receiver.

"I'm calling," he yells, "from our neighbor, two farms over, Madame Gosselin, who is the closest one in possession of a telephone!"

"I know this, Papa! How is . . . Maman?"

"Fine! Maman is fine! You have a new brother!"

"I do? A brother?" I press the phone tightly to my ear as hot tears roll down my face.

Rose heartily thumps my back. Then, un-Rose-like, she gives me some privacy, walking away, trailing the smell of the baby powder she always sprinkles on after her bath.

"Mathieu Gérard Luc Côté!" Papa continues loudly. "He was born early this morning, and he's small, just over six pounds, but he's healthy, Marie-Claire, he has all of his fingers and toes! Josée is so happy, she's already acting like a little mother, and she won't let him out of her sight! And soon you'll get to see him, too!"

"Yes, Papa!"

"I'll pick you up at St. Felix tomorrow, as you asked. But it still makes no sense to me that you are taking the train. Why would you want to do that for such a short distance? And your boyfriend—what's his name again?"

"It's Jack, Papa. Jack Hawkings."

"Hawkings. He's not French."

"No, Papa, he isn't French."

"Well, is he at least Catholic?"

"I never asked him."

"Ah me—so he's buying your ticket. And then he's going on to visit his family in Winnipeg?"

"Yes, Papa."

He pauses. "Well, you've always been stubborn, Marie-Claire. You have your own mind about things."

"Yes," I say again. "I'll see you soon. I can't wait!"

"Good, that's good," he says, his voice lifting once more.

At five-thirty the next evening, we're at the train. The conductor yells, *"Board!"* even though we are a small group and are standing close by and can clearly hear him.

Jack and I are the last ones on board. We move, with our packages, past the normal passengers. Some look at us and draw back slightly. Others pretend they haven't seen us and stare out at the snow.

We're TB patients, after all.

We find two seats at the back near the window, and Jack gives me my ticket. The heat from the corner wood-stove keeps everything warm, and there are festive frost patterns dancing up the glass. Yet as lovely as it is, and even though I'm finally going home for a while, my mind is back in the infirmary, where they'll have just delivered the evening meals. Signy will be sitting up in bed, trying to eat something.

Will she still be here next Christmas? Or the one after that?

I grip Jack's hand.

He turns to me, looks at my hand gripping his, then into my face, and he knows.

"It isn't too late to change your mind," he says.

"But you bought me this ticket."

"Cheap," he says with a little grin. "And I'll see you

after Christmas. And when I get to the station, I'll explain things to your dad."

"He'll be so angry!"

"He'll get over it."

The conductor comes by to take our tickets. He fingers Jack's, clips it, says, "Winnipeg," and then reaches out for mine.

"And you, young lady," he says, waiting, making conversation. "Going home for the holidays?"

I turn and throw my arms around Jack, and he kisses me and I kiss him back.

"Hurry," he whispers in my ear.

I break away and mumble "Sorry" to the startled conductor, and scramble to get out of my seat.

Next thing, I'm outside in the snow, running as hard as my TB will let me, flying as fast as my feet will take me, while behind me the train slowly pushes off and heads across the snowy prairie for St. Felix.

Acknowledgments

Thanks to the Manitoba Arts Council and the Canada Council for the Arts for your generous financial support. And to everyone at my Canadian and American publishers, Groundwood Books and Farrar Straus Giroux, and especially to Patsy Aldana, for your care and honesty.

Melanie and Shelley, this book is dedicated to you—no more needs to be said.

This book is a work of fiction. I drew from many sources during its research and development, among them the Manitoba Sanatorium, at Ninette in southwest Manitoba (on whose grounds my sister and I were raised as the kids of the medical superintendent), and its spiritual cousin, Trudeau Sanatorium, nestled in the Adirondack Mountains at Saranac Lake in upstate New York. Also very helpful were: TB memoirs and novels, in particular the stunning *Wish I Might*, by Isabel Smith Malmstrom, who was a patient at Trudeau Sanatorium for twenty-one years, until the development of TB drugs at the end of the Second World War led to her eventual cure; the evocative *Portrait of Healing: Curing in the Woods*, by Victoria E. Rinehart; and the detailed accounts of both Canadians and Americans during the war years in Barry Broadfoot's *Six War Years 1939–1945: Memories of Canadians at Home and Abroad* and Studs Terkel's *The Good War*.

Also invaluable were a large number of candid black-and-white photographs of the time that offered glimpses of ordinary lives caught in the extraordinary circumstances of sanatorium life. One in particular—of an unidentified tubercular boy, pathetically thin and flanked by his sad sisters—provided haunting inspiration for the Côté family.

I'm grateful to certain individuals for sharing with me their personal stories and impressions: Ada Bradford, Mary Houghton, Edith Vincent, Marilyn Hokanson, Stella Olver, Dr. Doreen Moggey, Dr. David Stewart and his wife Ruth, Dr. Alexander Pan, Jean Cross Farley, Helen Neufeld, Sally Beaufoy, my sister and brother-in-law Alice and Ed Drader, and Brian and Margaret Mackinnon.

More thanks than I can say to my husband, Brian Brooks, for the gift of his love and his constant ear, and to Maureen Hunter, Jeffrey Canton, and Sharon Jasper, for their unwavering friendship on this long journey.